Also By Heather Daughrity

Edited Anthologies

House of Haunts

Hospital of Haunts

Novels and Collections

Knock Knock

Tales My Grandmother Told Me

Echoes of the Dead: Collected Hauntings

Anthology Contributions (as Heather Miller)

These Lingering Shadows

The Horror Zine Magazine Fall, 2022

Into the Forest: Tales of the Baba Yaga

Tales from the Monoverse

Head Blown: Extreme Horror Stories

The Depths Unleashed, Volume One

The Horror Collection: Creature Feature Edition

Anthology Contributions (as Heather Daughrity)

Deathrealm: Spirits

The Monsters Next Door

Echoes of the Dead

Collected Hauntings

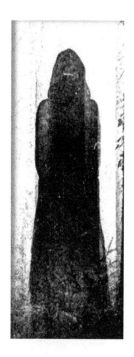

by

Heather Daughrity

Parlor Ghost Press

for all those who have ever grieved

and

for Joshua
whose love brought me back to life

Table of Contents

DESPAIR

Julia Marshall could count the moments of that fateful morning without thinking: a tragic movie playing in her head, moving scene by scene, horror mounting as the story moved toward its climax.

One. Her alarm went off at six-thirty. Julia rolled out of bed, pulled her hair up into a ponytail, did her morning workout, and took a quick shower.

Two. She roused her husband, Rich, with a kiss, then went to wake the children.

Three. She had breakfast on the table when Rich came downstairs, Mark and Holly trailing behind him. The children were dressed but still sleepy-eyed.

Four. Pancakes and bacon. Orange juice. Conversation. Laughter.

Five. She rushed the children through the rest of their preparations, packing folders and homework and brown-bagged lunches into their backpacks.

Six. She stood at the door, hair still damp from her shower, and kissed them each good-bye. Mark and Holly took off walking. This was their first year walking by themselves. Julia had been hesitant, but Rich had assured her that an eight- and ten-year-old were perfectly capable of walking on their own. Four blocks straight up to the elementary school. Two to Main Street, cross at the light, two more beyond.

Julia and Rich stood for a moment watching their children. The sun was bright. The birds were chirping. Mid-September meant the air was already warm at 7:45 in the morning.

Julia kissed her husband. He gave her backside a quick squeeze, wiggled his eyebrows. She laughed and swatted at him, sending him on his way.

Seven. Rich's car pulled out of the driveway, pointed north. Julia leaned forward out of the doorway. She could see Mark and Holly further down. If Rich hurried, he'd be able to wave at the kids while they all waited at the traffic light where their street met Main.

Eight. Everything went wrong.

The day was warm. She was already beginning to sweat along her hairline, salty drops trickling down the back of her neck. She would watch until the kids made it safely across Main Street, then go inside where the glorious air-conditioning would be her best friend for the rest of the day.

Julia stepped out onto the porch, rested her elbows on the railing, watched as the sun glinted off Holly's golden hair as the girl walked. The kids stopped at the intersection. Julia glanced up at the traffic light.

She squinted.

The light was out.

The children paused for a moment. From two blocks away, Julia could feel their uncertainty.

Rich's car approached them. He would help them. Signal when it was safe to cross.

The kids started on without him.

The red pickup truck driving west down Main did not stop. Did not slow.

The children crossed the midpoint of the street. Half a dozen more steps and they would have been safe. Mark realized what was happening, too late to change it. He stopped, frozen to the crosswalk. The boy threw an arm out in front of his little sister: one last heroic act.

The truck hit them.

Then kept going.

Julia was off the porch and running before the realization had time to solidify in her mind. Rich's car was ahead of her, tires screeching on the pavement as he pulled to a stop, halfway through the intersection.

His door opened. His feet and legs swung out. He stood.

The semi driving east slammed into Rich's car.

Julia ran. She did not feel the hot pavement that burned the soles of her feet nor the sprinkled glass which sliced them with a thousand pinprick cuts. She did not hear the shouts nor the incessant rumble of the eighteen-wheeler as she skirted the wreck.

Her eyes were focused, tunnel-visioned, on the two small forms which lay in the crosswalk. On the odd angles. The blood. The glassy eyes.

She screamed. She screamed until her throat bled, and she held the lifeless bodies, her children, one in each arm, pressed against her chest, while her eyes stared, both seeing and refusing to see, at her husband's head on the pavement ten feet away.

The dog days of summer rolled slowly into the crispness of autumn. The trees which surrounded the Marshall house blazed bright for a few weeks before carpeting the lawn with rich reds and oranges. Julia Marshall kept to herself. She slept odd hours, ate only when the hunger grew strong enough to hurt.

Mary Ann Malloy pushed her cart down the cereal aisle. She kept a discreet distance between them, but as she pretended to read the labels on the boxes before her, her eyes darted again and again to the woman a few feet further down.

Slowly, aisle by aisle, Mary Ann made her way through the store, always staying away, always just a corner behind, but always watching. She wasted a bit of time looking at the candy displays when the other woman went through the check-out, then hurried to put her groceries on the conveyor belt in the same lane.

Cheryl was Mary Ann's favorite cashier, because the two women were kindred spirits. They loved one thing above all else: gossip. And what better job to keep an eye on the comings and goings of the community than one where every single person in town had to pass by you regularly?

Cheryl scanned Mary Ann's items slowly, keeping an eye on the Julia Marshall's retreating back as she made her way out of the store and to the parking lot. As soon as Julia had cleared the supermarket doors, Cheryl turned, eyes shining.

"She did it again, didn't she?" Mary Ann asked, her voice low and conspiratorial.

"Yes!" Cheryl whispered.

"How long has it been now?" Mary Ann asked.

Cheryl counted on her fingers. "It happened last week of September, so… this is what? The fourth week since then?"

Mary Anne shook her head, watching through the large front windows as Julia loaded her groceries into the trunk of her car. She had first noticed it a couple of weeks ago, and had confirmed the situation with Cheryl: Julia Marshall was still buying groceries to feed her entire family.

Her entire *dead* family.

Every Monday, Julia filled her shopping cart with juice packs and pudding cups, sugary cereals and frozen pizzas. The exact same items each week. Mary Ann and Cheryl had checked.

Julia's car pulled out of the parking lot. Mary Ann shook her head again; Cheryl did the same.

"Still buying food for those kids. Poor woman. Something's not quite right in her head since it happened." Cheryl's look of sympathy did not quite hide the glint in her eye.

Mary Ann nodded. She slid her card through the reader and paid for her own groceries as Cheryl loaded the bags back into her cart. "I wonder if she actually cooks the food for them, too."

The first responders had come, of course. Police cars and fire trucks and ambulances, all blaring their horns and sirens, the cacophonous sound echoing off the buildings of Main Street in a never-ending round. A crowd had gathered, shopkeepers and morning commuters, and huddled in a group near the library, several schoolchildren who had the misfortune of passing the scene on their way to class.

Julia had clutched her children's bodies, shrieking and sobbing when kind but firm hands tried to take them from her. A parade of dark-blue pants above sturdy black boots passed to and fro around her, but Julia did not have the strength to lift her head to gaze above the knees of the men and women who took charge.

Traffic was rerouted, uniformed officers directing people away from Main, up the Hill, around the tragedy. There were many voices, many sounds, many flashing lights which disappeared into the brightness of the sun. And then, slowly, the crowd thinned. The sirens were shut off. The revolving red and blue lights ceased turning. The children were ushered off to school to be watched over by a harried counselor. The semi-truck was driven away. Rich's car was loaded onto the back of a tow truck.

Rich was placed, in three pieces – head, torso and upper legs, lower legs and feet – into a body bag.

At last, the street was cleared, everything taken away, everyone gone except for Julia Marshall, her children's bodies still clutched against her even as they stiffened, and a small group of firefighters and police officers who circled round her, shielding her from the curious eyes of passers-by.

Parked discreetly in the lot behind the library, the coroner's van waited.

Julia walked along the sidewalk. She did not rush nor did she shuffle too slowly; she had learned to keep herself at a steady pace lest people stop to ask if she was okay.

Autumn had finally arrived in full color. All around her blazed the red maples and the yellow birches and the fiery orange of the sweetgum trees.

Julia bent down to pick up one of the sweetgum seed pods – prickly balls, the kids had called them – which covered the path. She passed it from hand to hand as she walked, a magician who never quite mastered the trick of making something disappear.

She turned at Main Street. She had learned not to linger at the intersection, not to stare for minutes or hours at the dark stains which marred the white paint of the crosswalk or the tiny glistening diamonds of shattered glass ground into the pavement.

People stopped to talk to her if she did that, touching her on the arm or the shoulder, looking at her with pitying eyes that she wanted to gouge out with her fingernails. Yes, best not to linger.

She started down Main, the late afternoon sun at her back. The shops in the century-old buildings were decorated for Halloween. A life-sized Frankenstein's monster grinned and stretched his arms toward her from his slab. Pumpkins sat at every door. Billowing white-sheet ghosts swung back and forth on the breeze.

Taped up in the windows of every single store were flyers reminding people that the Main Street Trick or Treat was on Saturday at two o'clock.

"Oh, yes, trick or treat," Julia murmured, her lips barely moving. "Holly, what do you want to be again?"

You remember, Mom. I wanted to be a dragon this year. And Mark wanted to be a ninja. Again.

"That's right. Dragon and ninja. Dragon and ninja." Julia walked down the street, skirting fallen leaves and leftover candy wrappers from the previous weekend's parade. People stepped out of her way as she mumbled.

But Mom, we can't trick or treat this year.

"Dragon and ninja. Dragon and ninja."

Mom, we're dead, don't you remember?

Julia shuddered, wrapped her arms around herself, kept walking.

"Dragon and ninja. Dragon and ninja."

In the end, the paramedics pried Julia's cramped fingers from the bodies of her children. Their bodies were laid gently on top of open bags, tucked in, zipped up, carried away. Julia sat and stared at the places they had just been until the paramedics returned to lift her from the ground. Her body contracted, legs drawing up, arms tucking in, a subconscious protecting of the womb in which her children had grown.

A pain, sharp, cramping, and unbearable, pierced though her. She cried out, an inhuman sound. She spasmed in the grasp of the EMTs who held her, then vomited her long-ago breakfast onto the pavement and all over their shoes.

Then Julia Marshall's body flushed from head to toe, the world went blurry around her, her eyes rolled back, and her body went limp. A blessed darkness settled in.

Julia had been medicated, drugged into a passive oblivion. Her sister, Jen, drove in from Arkansas and oversaw the necessary preparations.

The triple funeral was held on a sunny Saturday morning, the first leaves on the trees in the cemetery just starting to show edges of autumn color. Julia stood in her black dress, dark glasses covering her unfocused eyes, and watched as three coffins – one large, two heartbreakingly small – were lowered into the ground.

Jen led her sister back to the car, back to the house. There were people everywhere. Food was heaped upon the dining table and the kitchen counters. A thousand quiet voices lulled Julia into a trance.

Half an hour into the reception, she slipped quietly upstairs to her bedroom, shut the door, kicked off her shoes, stripped off her dress, laid down on her bed, and slept through the rest of the day and the night that followed.

Jen stayed on for a few more days and then left, off to Arkansas and her own living, breathing children. Julia stood on the front porch and watched her sister leave. She hugged the soft arms of her bathrobe tight around her, a straitjacket against the pain.

Jen's car slowed at the traffic light on Main. The light worked now, its colors bright against a backdrop of storm clouds moving in from the northwest. Julia's eyes followed the circles of color as they changed: yellow, red, green. Jen turned the corner, headed east toward the highway, and was gone.

An hour later, Julia still stood in the same place, eyes fixed to the lights two blocks away.

Yellow, red, green. Yellow, red, green.

On the first Saturday of December, Julia Marshall dragged in seven tubs of Christmas decorations and the unwieldy box containing the artificial Christmas tree.

That tree had been a real bone of contention during the first few years of their marriage; Julia had always grown up with the real thing, but Rich wanted the convenience of a fake one. She had acquiesced, and eventually she had gotten used to it. She still missed the fragrance of a good fir tree, though.

It took her the better part of the day to put everything out. She had some trouble circling the lights around the tree – that had always been a two-person job before, but in the end she got it done.

She plugged in all the strands, first to each other and finally to the wall outlet. Then she flipped the switch on the wall down.

Shining out through the sudden darkness, the living room was bathed in a rainbow of lights, not only those on the tree but also strands strung along the windows and doorways. Julia sat on the couch and looked contentedly around her.

"Do you like it, guys? Did I do a good job?"

Yes, Mom. Mark's voice this time, echoing around the room.

"You guys still need to make your Christmas lists. What do you want this year? There's only a few weeks left to shop."

We don't want anything, Mom. We're dead.

Julia slapped her hands against her thighs, hard. She laughed, a sound just this side of sanity. "I guess it will just have to be a surprise then!"

Julia stretched her body out along the couch. She lay facing the dancing lights of the Christmas tree. Her eyes grew heavy; the lights began to blur. Julia watched as they changed colors.

Yellow, red, green. Yellow, red, green.

Dave stepped up on the running board of the #3 garbage truck and gave the side a couple of good knocks. Travis revved the engine, shifted the truck into gear, and pulled forward. They had just finished Fifth Street; the rising sun hit Dave's eyes as they turned the corner and began the long, slow haul up Sixth.

When they got to the Marshall house, Dave approached the bins with a feeling of both sadness and hope. Sadness at what they had found in the bins every week for months now; hope that this might be the week they didn't.

He let out a sigh. The winter cold was at least keeping the stench to a minimum. If she kept this up into the warmer months, all the spoiled food would stink to high heaven.

Dave glanced up at the house. All the windows were still dark; most houses were this early in the morning, but he had a feeling that Julia Marshall didn't keep regular hours like most folks. He half expected to see her standing at the window watching him.

Sure that no one was looking, he lifted the top bag from the bin. Same thing as always. Frozen pizzas gone soggy, a jug of curdling milk, bags and boxes still full of cookies and crackers. Poor Mrs.

Marshall. He pitied her, he truly did. He wondered if she had any close friends or some family who were keeping an eye on her.

Something wasn't quite right with her since that terrible accident a few months back. Not that a person ever could be quite right after something like that. A shame, it was. And the most bizarre thing he'd witnessed in all his fifty years.

Dave dropped the bag back into the bin, walked over to the controls on the side of the truck, pressed the buttons that made the truck's long arm slide around the bin and hoist it into the air, dumping its contents in among the rest of Harrisville's trash.

He made sure the bin was properly set back on the grass near Mrs. Marshall's curb, gave one last pitying look up at the dark house, then stepped up onto the truck and motioned for Travis to move on to the next spot.

January proved a hard month for Julia. Weeks of freezing rain made the house a dark and chilled prison from which she could not escape. She padded about with her warmest robe pulled over her flannel pajamas, two pairs of socks on her constantly freezing feet.

The darkness and the water streaming incessantly down the windows made her feel claustrophobic, like the world beyond was disappearing altogether and only she, alone in that big old house, still remained, floating in a black void of space beneath one enormous never-ceasing raincloud.

Shadows stretched long in those days. There never seemed to be enough light to reach the corners of the rooms, and the stairwell and upstairs hall were lost in perpetual twilight.

It was during those long, cold, dark days that Julia began to hear them. Of course, she'd been hearing their voices in her head every day since she stopped taking the meds her doctor had prescribed. But she *knew* that was in her head, knew that was only her children's memories trapped in her brain cells, rattling around along her dendrites, ricocheting off the soft pink folds of her cerebral matter like ping-pong balls.

This was something different.

At night as she lay in bed, she heard them moving. Footsteps in the hall. Thumps against the wall. Doors opening and closing. But every time she got up to look, there was nothing there. The house would go silent but for the steady rattle of rain and hail on the metal roof.

She would see little signs of them around the house. Rich's shoes shifted just slightly from their place in the mudroom. Mark's Rubik's Cube, still sitting squarely on the edge of the desk in the game room, but with the little colored squares switched, red where green should be, blue instead of yellow.

Holly's colored pencils, normally arrayed in perfect rows on the drawing table in her bedroom, would be tilted at odd angles, as if the little girl had been right there just a moment before, as if she had gotten up quickly from her small chair and skipped away, knocking a few pencils out of line just as her mother walked into the room.

Julia began sleeping in her children's rooms, on a nest of blankets, trying to catch them at their midnight play. But she always seemed to be in the wrong room, and the endless hours of the night became a game of hide-and-seek as she followed their footsteps and laughter from one end of the house to the other.

She just wanted to *see* them, to see Mark's lopsided grin and run her hand through Holly's golden curls. She wanted her husband, too, wanted to wrap her arms around his waist and lay her head against his chest and go back, back to the way things were, back before that day (she could count the moments: *one, two, three, four, five…*), back to when she wasn't so goddamned alone all the time.

Julia woke up in strange places. She might go to sleep in Holly's room and wake up in the bathtub or drift off on Mark's floor and startle awake with the first rays of sunlight to find herself perched precariously on one of the kitchen stools, her head on her arms, resting on the bar countertop. She knew something was wrong, knew that her head wasn't quite right these days. But she just wanted to see them. She wanted it so much.

Helen Graves stood at her bedroom window, looking out into the yard next door. She clucked her tongue in disapproval. "She's doing it again, Reg," she said, addressing her husband, who was still in bed, in his pajamas.

"And?" he asked, and even without turning around, Helen knew that he was giving her the look, the one that said that she ought to be minding her own business and not spying on her neighbors. She wasn't a busybody, she really wasn't, not like that Cheryl down at the market, but it was hard not to notice when your own neighbor did something as strange as this.

Helen ignored Reg's pointed throat-clearing and continued watching the woman in the back yard next to theirs. The Marshalls had been a nice family; Helen had liked them from the moment they moved in six years ago. Julia Marshall had always been a quiet one, but pleasant enough. The Marshalls kept their house and yard neat and clean and taught their children manners, and that made them okay with Helen.

But poor Julia.

Helen had first noticed it back in the fall. She happened to be passing by the window on the way to putting her laundry away when she noticed Julia out next door, hanging her own laundry on the line. That was another thing Helen liked about Mrs. Marshall. She tended to do things the old-fashioned way.

Helen had paused just for a moment, a swelling of sympathy rising in her chest for her neighbor who had been through so much. Then she had stepped closer to the window, her brows furrowed in confusion as she got a good look at exactly what Julia was hanging on the line.

Mr. Marshall's work shirts. Little T-shirts, small dresses. Socks no adult foot could ever fit into.

Helen had tried to rationalize it at first. Maybe Julia was doing some cleaning, a part of the grieving process, going through everyone's things, giving them one last good wash and dry before packing them off to either the Salvation Army or to sit in boxes up in the attic until she was ready to part with them.

But when the next week, and the next week, and the next after that had found Helen watching out the window again, and Julia hanging the *exact* same clothes out on the line, rational reasoning went out the door.

Helen had watched her neighbor hang out the same clothes – even hanging them in the exact same order in the exact same place on the line – each week until the weather grew too cold.

She had a sneaking suspicion that Julia was probably still hanging those same clothes on lines strung up across the garage all through the winter, and she had been eagerly anticipating the first nice weather of the year just to see if Julia would reappear with her basket full of clothes belonging to her dead family.

And she had.

"There's something not quite right with her, you know. I'm worried about her, Reg. Reg?"

Helen turned around, but her husband had already left the room. She turned back to the window and gazed down as Julia hung a pale-yellow dress on the line. Helen shook her head and murmured to herself.

"Something not quite right at all."

Things had progressed. They were there, in the house with her. Julia was sure of it now. She had proof.

She had *seen* them.

They were only shadows at first, quick flashes of movement that most people would miss. But not Julia. She was always vigilant, always watching, always waiting to catch the slightest sign that they were with her.

And then the shadows took on substance, took on color, became something more.

The first time Julia saw them and knew – *knew* – that her children had come back to her was at the end of a day like so many others before it. She had wandered the rooms of the house aimlessly, sat in front of the television without seeing it, picked up and put down half a dozen books without reading a word.

It was a Sunday – she remembered because she had just come inside from carrying out several large bags of trash. It seemed like she had so much trash these days. The kids just didn't eat much anymore. They must be going through a phase.

So, she had dumped the bags into the garbage bins and walked back inside, closing the back door behind her, and as she turned to face the kitchen, she saw it. The trailing end of a skirt disappeared around the corner of the doorway where the kitchen met the back hall. Julia stood for a moment, afraid to move, afraid to breathe, afraid to believe what she had just seen but unable to tamp down the hope that now rose inside her.

Slowly, cautiously, she walked forward, craning her neck to see around the edge of the doorframe.

Nothing.

But something, some feeling deep inside her, a healthy dose of mother's intuition, told her to keep going. Julia walked silently through the dark back hall and into the dining room. Up ahead, a flash of blue fabric led her on, through the living room and to the bottom of the front stairs. Up above, all was darkness. Julia waited, one foot on the bottom stair, peering upward, searching for any sign of movement.

She felt pulled, as if an invisible string were attached somewhere in the region of her aching, empty womb and someone – or something – at the top of the stairs was carefully tugging her forward.

Julia made her way up, stopping every few steps, listening, waiting, watching. When she reached the top she stood in the middle of the hall, turning her head slightly from side to side. The anticipation which had built up inside her began to dissipate, the static prickling of the air fading away. Julia stood until her legs began to cramp, then she allowed herself to slide to the floor, her back against the wall, and she cried.

A few days later, she saw Holly again. A glint of light caught Julia's eye as she walked from room to room, placing neatly folded stacks of laundry on everyone's beds. When she looked up, she saw her daughter, sitting hunched up in the corner of her bedroom, her hands over her face, her hair shining in the glow from the overhead light.

Julia had carefully set down the laundry basket, and even more carefully approached her daughter. As she drew nearer, she could hear it: the slightest, barely-there sound of the child's sobs. Julia stretched out her hand toward Holly, but stopped just before touching her, fingers mere inches away.

"Holly, honey, what's wrong?" Julia whispered, sure that any sound louder than a breath would make her daughter fade away.

The answer seemed to come from everywhere all at once, her daughter's voice, quiet and yet somehow inescapable as it circled the walls of the room.

"I don't like the dark, Mommy. Why is it so dark?"

Julia had paused, confused. She glanced around. It was daytime, sunlight coming clearly through the pale purple curtains that covered her daughter's windows. It wasn't dark at all.

When she turned back to ask Holly what she meant, the girl was gone.

It wasn't until later that day, when the sun began to set, that Julia realized what Holly must have meant. She had become so used to walking the house in darkness all through the hours of the night that she had almost forgotten that they used to always leave the light on in the upstairs hall. Julia flipped the switch upward, soft yellow light illuminating the corridor, pushing all the shadows away into the corners.

"Here, baby. No more darkness. You don't have to be afraid. Come back, please."

Holly had not come back that night.

The next time Julia saw them, they were together, Mark and Holly, her babies. She had been lying in bed, meaning to sleep but in truth alternately staring at the ceiling fan overhead and allowing her eyes to close and her mind to go numb, when she heard the sudden and unmistakable sound of water splashing.

Her heart pounding in her ears, Julia rose from the bed and made her way across the hall – the light still shining brightly – to the bathroom door. The sounds were louder here, splashes punctuated with giggles. She pushed the door open slowly, willing it not to creak.

They were both there, dressed in their swimsuits, one at each end of the big, deep tub. Mark had his snorkel on and was splashing water at Holly, who was shrieking with glee. Julia stood, one hand on the doorknob, her heart aching and her throat burning with the tears she choked back, and simply watched them.

Both children turned toward her at the same time. Mark's eyes were huge, magnified behind the glass of his face mask.

"Mommy," he said, and his voice sounded strange, distorted, muffled through the tube of the snorkel which he still held in his mouth.

"Oh, baby," Julia said, a whimper, a prayer.

"Come play with us, Mommy." Mark's voice sounded even stranger now, distant. Julia had the sudden fear that he was being pulled away from her, the distance from the bathroom door to the tub stretching out longer and longer in front of her with each second.

She stumbled forward, reached out for her children, leaped across the last few feet of the puddled floor to land, feet-first, in the tub. She sank to her knees, warm water soaking through her pants, spreading her arms out to either side to embrace her babies, her loves. Both children leaned toward her, their small hands reaching upward, and then…

Julia fought her way up out of the water, coughing, spluttering. She was alone in the bathtub, fully clothed, fully submerged, in water which had grown bone-chillingly cold.

She heaved herself over the side of the tub, soaked, gasping for air, hot tears flowing freely down her face, mixing with the frigid water that streamed down from her dripping hair.

She did not see her children again for weeks after that.

But she did not give up hope.

Not yet.

The windows were open. A day which felt like May even though it was March had warmed the many rooms of the house, and now as the sky turned pink with the sun's descent, a soft breeze had risen, sending dead leaves scuttling along the sidewalk outside and causing the sheer curtains within to float and fall in time with the wind's swells.

She liked the feel of the air circulating around her, the way the floors felt cool beneath her bare feet and the way the loose strands of her hair lifted with the current. She'd felt cooped up these last few weeks; ice and snow and anxiety had kept her indoors, the sky a perpetual gray that seemed to mirror her own state of mind.

Today, though, had been a nice reprieve from the cold and the overcast skies; today had been a literal breath of fresh air, and though the twilit evening was quickly dropping off into the edge of true nighttime darkness and the warmth of the day was evaporating with the disappearance of the sun, still she kept the windows open, still she let the crisp eddies of air move through the stuffy rooms of the house, still she closed her eyes and breathed in deeply, as if hoping that by taking in enough of the clean air she could somehow cleanse her spirit of its recent grief.

She no longer worried about things like making sure the doors were locked or checking that the gates were properly fastened. Every window in the house being open to the darkness might once have caused her a great deal of anxiety, especially being there all alone, but her mind had stopped fretting over such things

Danger did not concern her anymore. The thought of pain, of fear, of death, did not cause the slightest trouble in her mind. Everything, every person, every purpose worth living for, worth caring about, had been taken from her.

If the reaper himself had walked into her bedroom at that very moment, she thought, *she would have stood calmly, put aside the book she was reading, and walked happily, numbly, into his welcome embrace.*

In truth she was not actually reading the book. She had held it, open to the same page, for several minutes now. She had settled herself into the chair in her bedroom with the book some time before – an hour, perhaps, or more, when there was still enough light coming through the window behind her to illuminate the words, though her eyes must have scanned the same paragraph a hundred times without knowing what she was seeing.

Now that full darkness had settled, she could barely make out the lines of text against the background of the page.

The light in the upstairs hall was on. It was always on, had always been on since that day when Holly had cried out that she didn't like the dark.

Of course, it had always been on when Holly was alive. They had left it on so that if one of the children needed to get up – to go to the bathroom, to get a drink, to seek out their parents after a bad dream – they would be able to see where they were going.

Julia had a great fear, when they first moved in, that one of the children – or perhaps even she, herself – might go stumbling in the darkness of the hall and straight into the opening at the top of the stairs, down that steep incline to the floor of the entryway below.

She had no such fears now. She could find her way through that house in utter darkness if she needed to. She had lived in that utter darkness for months after the accident, preferring it to the light that revealed too much empty space. But she hadn't switched off the light since Holly's cries had echoed around her. She wouldn't do that to her baby.

She hadn't changed a single thing since that day, the day when everything was taken from her.

In the pink room at one end of the hallway, her daughter's stuffed animals still sat in anticipation of a game that would never resume. In the green room at the other end, model planes hung, swaying in the breeze, over an unmade bed and a pile of candy wrappers that her son would never throw away.

There on the floor, just to the side of her dresser, a dark shape that she knew to be her husband's pajamas, dropped there in his hurry to get going on that fateful day, still sat, untouched.

She couldn't bear to think of them, of her family, but could bear even less the thought of somehow erasing their last moments from the memory of the house.

So, things remained, just as they had been. She shopped from the same grocery list every week, the paper it was written on now creased, the writing beginning to fade. She washed the same load of laundry, the clothing now piled back into the basket, waiting for the next washing day.

She was sitting in the darkness now, the triangle of yellow light from the hall spilling into her bedroom but not quite reaching her. Her eyes were closed, her breathing slow and steady. She was listening carefully to all the myriad sounds that drifted in through the windows: the creaking of the branches of the trees along the side of the house, the distant sound of cars in town, the call of some bird – confused perhaps by the warm late-winter day, the long, mournful whistle of a train passing by in the night.

The slamming of the door made her jump, upset her carefully crafted peace of mind. Her eyes flew open as an annoyed breath huffed out of her nostrils. The bathroom door, just across the hall, had shut.

It was obviously the breeze that had done it, the wind creating conflicting drafts throughout the house, and rather than being unnerved, she was simply irritated by this intrusion of sound and movement on her otherwise serene environment.

She stood up, crossed the hall, opened the bathroom door. It was colder within, the night air filling up the small room, the white tiles absorbing the chill and reflecting it back at her as she stood motionless in the center of the floor, goosebumps prickling the bare skin of her arms.

She would have sighed, had she wanted to expend the extra energy; instead, she closed the bathroom window in silence, then proceeded around the house, walking from the light of the hall into the darkness of the bedrooms and back again, closing windows as she went.

She stepped slowly but lightly down the stairs to the main rooms of the first floor, closing the windows there, too, till the house was sealed up once more like the tomb she knew it to be, and then she returned to her bedroom, to sit once more in her chair, her book forgotten completely, dropped onto the floor next to her, facedown, its spine creased, its title unreadable in the darkness.

Ten minutes passed, her mind lulled by the steady hum of the central heat now escaping through the air vents in the ceiling, lulled almost into sleep, or that thing which passed for sleep in the life she now found herself living.

The door slammed again.

Her eyes opened; the rest of her body remained completely still. Her gaze locked on the bathroom door across the hall. Her heart, having skipped a beat or two at the first startling of the sound, dropped back into its steady rhythm as she stared, curious, at the four panels set into the door, at the glass doorknob against its brass plate.

At the light reflecting off the doorknob as it turned.

A quick inhalation of breath, and she leaned forward a few inches, eyes squinted as she focused on the knob.

Turning, turning, frustratingly slowly, until she heard it: the click as the latch disengaged.

Then the creak as the door opened inward; one inch, two inches, then a clear stop as if it had come up against something solid.

She stood, shaking with anticipation and adrenaline, with a fear of and hope for something she dared not name, and stepped forward, her feet moving from the plush carpet of her bedroom to the smooth wooden boards of the hallway, her hand reaching out in front of her toward that doorknob to grasp it...

Every door in the house slammed shut at once.

Her hand, inches from the bathroom door, jerked back reflexively, and she cradled it against her chest with her other hand as if it had been injured. She turned where she stood, her eyes roving from one closed door to another: the bathroom, her daughter's room, her own bedroom, the hall closet, her son's room, a complete circle of the upper floor.

Behind her, a creak sounded as Mark's door opened. A few inches at first, a pause, then more, until the door stood half ajar. A shifting of the shadows within, a silhouette, a recognition half-formed, the exact height, the exact shape of...

No. Julia took a step back, stopped suddenly as the door to her daughter's room let out its own familiar squeak. Her eyes darted toward it. Light from the streetlamp beyond bathed the room in a hazy amber glow.

She watched as small fingers gripped the edge of the door, and her heart gave a thump so hard she bent forward in pain. The top of a head appeared, golden hair shining in the light, one blue eye peering out as if her daughter were about to jump out, giggling, and shout *peek-a-boo!*

She saw movement in front of her, a flash of light in the dark bathroom as the shape of her husband scraped a straight razor over stubble, the metal reflecting back the hall light as it slid up and down, up and down.

To her left, the light of the hallway dimmed as the shadow of her son emerged from his room, footsteps like empty echoes on the wooden floor. To her right, as the light flickered, in jolting movements her daughter's form jerked toward her. In front of her, the bathroom door opened further, and her husband's heavier tread joined that of her children as they moved closer, surrounding her.

Come with us, Mommy. Her daughter's voice sounded in her head though the shadow in front of her did not open its mouth.

Come on, Mom, you don't want to stay here all alone, do you? The shape that was almost her son tilted its head as his voice filled her mind.

The silhouette in front of her stepped forward, spoke in her husband's voice: *Come along, darling.*

Her family! They were here! They couldn't be, she knew this, knew with certainty and finality that they were buried beneath six feet of cold dirt in the cemetery just outside of town, and yet they were here, with her, and they wanted…

A clammy fear gripped her heart as she looked at the converging shadows. A twisting vine of icy apprehension pooled around her bare feet and circled up her legs. She shivered violently.

"Oh, my loves!" she sobbed, and she reached out toward the thing that both was and was not her son.

A bloodred flame erupted in the recesses where his eyes should have been, and she snatched her hand back in pain as a low rumbling laughter filled the air, vibrating the floorboards beneath her.

"What? No." Her voice was a hoarse whisper, barely discernible over the rising laughter and a wind which came from nowhere and rushed through the house, unnatural and biting cold.

Julia shook her head, trying to dislodge the vision, the feeling, the awful nightmare that this must be. Her stomach clenched, not in fear but in grief, in sorrow, in anguish at the loss that she had kept herself numb to for months, a torment that rose suddenly within her, a dirge of pain and despair so strong it drowned out the laughter and the wind, the shadows wavering before her, these shadows of her own loss, these apparitions of her own consuming sadness, these harbingers of the darkness she had kept so long at bay.

Come with us, Mommy.

She looked at the staticky shape which was not her daughter but spoke with her daughter's voice, and she knew, deep inside her, that no happiness existed in this world for her any longer, knew that the things worth living for had deserted her, knew that life was too much, too long, too horribly empty to endure for another year, another month, another day.

"Yes," she said, knees buckling beneath her.

"No," she said, stumbling backward.

"My loves," she said, as her foot came down behind her into the empty space at the top of the stairs.

"My darlings."

Her last words came out as a whisper as her body went, head over heels, down the steep staircase. Her head hit the tiled floor at the bottom with an undeniably lethal crack. Her sight swam in and out of focus. Pain pierced every part of her body.

Above her, at the top of the stairs, the hall light flickered. Shadows gathered, two, then three, joining together into the horror that was a mother's worst nightmare: her grief come to life before her eyes. The shadow swooped down upon her, pressing its impenetrable darkness against her, until she could see nothing, hear nothing, feel nothing.

Thirty Years Later

"What's the story with that house?" the couple asked.

The realtor followed their line of sight to the house on the corner, its paint peeling, roof sagging, yard overgrown. She sighed. That eyesore drove down the property values of the entire neighborhood and scared away prospective buyers of the surrounding homes.

"A real tragedy, that," she said, unlocking the door to the house she was supposed to be showing them. "The bank owns the house, has for years. No one wants to put in the work to fix it up."

The man's eyes stayed locked on the old house. His wife looked up at him curiously.

"Is it for sale, though?" he asked.

The realtor sighed. "It could be." She hoped he'd leave it at that.

"I bet you could get it for a steal, though, couldn't you? Take the money you saved and put it into restoring it. I bet it'd be a real beauty with a little TLC."

The realtor shook her head. "You really don't want to go getting mixed up with that house. Trust me."

"Why?" the man asked, giving her what she supposed he thought was a charming grin. "Is it haunted or something?"

"Or something," the realtor responded, but the man's grin just grew wider.

"Ooh," he said, and his wife giggled. "Tell me more."

The realtor crossed her arms across her chest and stared at the house in question. "Fine," she said. "Years ago, a family lived there. There was an accident one day, as the father was going to work and the kids to school – a horrible car crash just a few blocks down. The dad and the kids were killed instantly."

"Oh, that's sad," the wife said, but the husband gestured for the realtor to continue.

"The wife – the mother – seemed to be okay. Well, as okay as you can be in that situation. She sat through the funeral, the graveside service. Let everyone in town shake her hand and pat her back and express their condolences. Then she went home and sort of locked herself away for a while. No one thought much about it, no one wanted to disturb her grieving.

"Then one day, when someone finally did stop by, there was no answer. They could just make out her shape through the lacy curtains that covered the front windows. The police were called, the door broken down. She'd been dead for a while at that point, a couple of weeks at least. She was at the foot of the stairs, body broken, head at an unnatural angle.

"Some people thought it was an accident. Some people thought she threw herself down the stairs in a fit of grief. They say she hadn't changed a thing in the house since her family died. Their breakfast dishes from that day, still sitting on the table with the leftover food rotted onto them. Clothes still in the hamper. Toys still strewn about. Sad, disturbing stuff.

"Well," – the realtor took a deep breath before she continued – "after a few months, the house went back to the bank. It was sold several times, for less and less each time, but no one ever stayed long. They say… they say the doors open and close on their own. That cold breezes blow through the house even in the summer. That a woman – or the shape of a woman – appears sometimes on the stairs, and that sometimes people feel pushed near the top, as if something is trying to make them fall. But mostly… mostly they just hear crying. The crying of a grief-stricken mother."

The realtor shivered at her own story.

The man looked thoughtfully up at the old house. "I think we'll chance a ghost for a good deal, won't we, babe?" He put his arm around his wife and pulled her close.

The realtor shrugged. "I'll see what I can do about finding a key if you really want to check it out. But it won't be today. I'll have to make some calls first."

The man rubbed his stubbly chin with one hand for a moment before answering. "That's alright. You see what you can do. Let us know when we can get in to see it. I don't mind putting in a little work on a house, do you, babe?"

His wife shook her head.

"And I don't mind a ghost or two, as long as she keeps quiet while the game is on!" The man laughed and led his wife away down the sidewalk toward their car.

The realtor watched them drive away. She let her gaze wander back to the old house. In the nearest upper window, a curtain fluttered, as if someone had stood looking out and had just walked away, letting it drop. The realtor stared for a moment longer, then shook her head and hurried to her car.

Upstairs in the old house, just beyond the window, a shape that both was and was not a grieving mother hung weightless in the air, a shadow on the wall, a loss given shape, a sorrow given form.

I HELD A LIFE

I once held a life in my hands.

Seven weeks gestation,
  almost.
Six weeks and five days.

Some say: *fetus*,
Some say: *baby*.
I called it my child.

I birthed it with blood and pain
Though far less than there would have been
Had this tiny creature survived longer.

I held it in my hands;
Not even both hands, but one hand.
One palm cupped the entirety of this child's being,

Echoes of the Dead

Preserved perfectly in a membranous bubble
Of fluid.

We tried for so many years.
I cried such ugly tears.

This perfect little human-tadpole.
Eyes, spine,
Tiny whorls where ears should grow.
Nubs for arms and legs and even tinier nubs, fanned out,
That might one day have been fingers holding tight to mine.

I had to call out to one of my older children:
Bring me the phone, please.
I had to call my husband at work:
I'm losing the baby. Come quick, please.
I had to call my doctor:
What do I do? Help me, oh, please.

The bathroom smelled of copper and iron,
Of the blood that rushed out,
Of the flood that pushed that child from my body.

No matter how many times I scrubbed and bleached and wept,
The smell remained.
A phantom, perhaps, in my nostrils.
That tiny bathroom a tomb, haunted.

I held a life in my body,
I held a life in my hands.

A thing so precious, so sacred, that just to look upon it seemed both
blessing and sacrilege.

The doctor probed inside me, watched the images on the screen.
Completely empty.
Completely
Empty.

It is okay to cry, she said.
It is good to cry.
That was your child that died, and it is
Okay to mourn him.
She hugged me and patted my shoulder.
I had no words to speak back to her.

For months the tears came.
Morning, noon, dead of night.
Then the pain receded, little by little.
It became lighter, less, easier,
Till the pain itself was a phantom
Haunting back corners of my mind.

November ninth.
Twelve years ago this year.
The pain still glides, specter-like,
Within me.

No grave marks that child's resting place,
The enormous loss too small to merit.
But each year I pick fresh flowers from
My garden

Echoes of the Dead

(Silk flowers too gaudy, too cheap an offering),
Fresh flowers grown by my own hand
As the child grew in my own body.
These I take and place beside my grandmother's grave
(She who lost five children of her own, and shares the knowledge of
this depth of sorrow),
In memory

Of a life denied,
A life mourned.

I held my child in one palm,
Its weight like feathers, like air.
Its weight like stones that crushed me,
that drove me to my knees.

DUALITY

Caleb Patton sat up slowly; there was a trick to this act, a specific way things had to be done. Getting the top half upright, that was the hardest part. Then swinging the legs over the side of the bed, which was not so much swinging as fighting against the pull of the sheets with tired legs attached to aching hips.

Once he managed to get his feet hanging down, inches from the floor, there was the slow scooting forward along the mattress until his toes touched the cold tile below. Then the big push, the surge of energy needed to draw his entire body vertical, feet planted firmly, one hand holding to the bedrail, the other stretched out to the side like a tightrope walker fighting to maintain balance.

He stood for a moment, waiting while the room settled around him, before sliding his feet into the soft familiar comfort of his slippers.

Marie would be in soon, he knew, and if she caught him out of bed on his own, she'd wag her finger at him and remind him yet again how dangerous it was to do absolutely anything without help.

But he didn't need her help, not really, not for most things, and certainly not for what he intended to do before this day was over.

Ten years earlier

The Golden Boys of Gideon, that's what people called them.

Caleb and Colton Patton, twins, each blessed with the envied trifecta of good looks, athletic skills, and sharp intelligence. Mix in quick wits, kind hearts, and easy charm, and the Patton twins were shining examples of everything young men should be.

The girls at Gideon High wanted to date them; the boys wanted to *be* them.

As the end of their senior year approached, the brothers found themselves much sought after, both by colleges hoping to offer them athletic scholarships and by giggling young ladies hoping for prom dates.

The college question was easy enough. They'd go, together, to their father's alma mater.

The prom question presented more of an opportunity for reflection and discussion.

So many girls, so little time.

But eventually, choices were made. Two starry-eyed hopefuls found their dreams coming true; another hundred found their own hopes crushed.

On the night of the big dance, Caleb and Colton took turns straightening each other's bowties, making sure each hair was held perfectly in place, and jokingly encouraging one another to add more, more, and more cologne.

The night went predictably enough.

They picked up their dates, Caleb up front with Melanie Rose, Colton folding himself into the back with Ginny. The high school gym was festooned in streamers, the basketball goals almost hidden behind great bunches of balloons.

The Golden Boys of Gideon made the rounds, grinning their Cheshire-cat grins, shaking hands, thumping their buddies on the back. They graciously kissed the hands of all the girls they'd turned down as the young men who'd scooped up their leftovers stood by, glowering. Ginny and Melanie Rose trailed along behind them, feet already aching in their high-heeled shoes, just happy to bask in the edges of the brothers' spotlight.

They laughed, they danced, they drank punch.

The prom ended at ten, but everyone knew that the real fun happened afterward.

Two hours later, the couples climbed back into their car. The brothers were flushed with alcohol and swagger; their dates giggled through a tipsy haze as they adjusted their dresses and patted their hair back into place.

The girls were dropped off, but the boys didn't go straight home. They had a six-pack each in the trunk, and they intended to salute this final rite of teenage passage properly.

There was a spot on the outskirts of town, a place reached via a gravel road that ran along the edge of Highback Ridge before veering off into the woods.

The boys had loved this secret hideaway since they were children. They had spent many hours playing there, hidden from their parents and the rest of the world. More recently, they'd gone there to think and plan and dream, to talk through all the possible paths their future might take.

And it was always "future," not "futures." The idea that at some point their lives might diverge, that they might take roads which led in different directions, had never occurred to them.

So, with the future stretching out ahead of them, the boys took this one last night to linger over the past, with all its accomplishments and accolades.

They drank as they drove, the night sky warm and open above them.

They drove quickly, recklessly, on the empty back-country roads.

They made it to their secret spot.

They did not make it home.

The last thing Caleb remembered was the way the stars spun. The sky was full of them, a thousand shimmering silver points against a black backdrop.

He'd been looking up when it happened, his mind blissfully relaxed, his concentration caught somewhere between the heaviness of his body in the passenger seat and the free-floating oblivion of space.

"Look," he'd said. "Colton. Look at the stars."

The spinning shifted, the stars held for the briefest moment in motionless stasis before rushing, faster than light, in the other direction.

Caleb felt his body moving, sliding and jerking, his neck stretching in impossible ways as he tried to keep an eye on the night sky while the car spun out, as Colton's shouts filled his ears, as they skidded across the gravel, slammed through the flimsy barrier, and crashed uncontrollably down the steep incline of Highback Canyon.

The first thing he noticed was the incessant beeping. His body felt numb, his brain sluggish. His eyes fought against the heavy sand that held them closed, opening a crack and then closing again quickly as burning light reached his retinas.

He tried again – slowly, squinting.

The world came into focus little by little. The glowing numbers on the machine next to his bed, the tubes which ran from that machine to some place hidden beneath the blue blanket that covered him. A clock on the wall. Beneath it, a crucifix.

The sound of a door opening made him turn his head, a reflexive movement which he immediately regretted. Pain erupted over him like lava, a burning, flowing, aching agony that made him gasp. His entire body tensed, fresh waves of torment coursing through every nerve. He heard himself moaning, hated the sound but could not stop it.

Quick footsteps approached him. Through the haze of light and pain he saw a nurse appear at the side of his bed, a look of concern on her face.

"Oh, dear," she murmured, pushing buttons on the loud machine, miraculously silencing it. She reached above her, checking something which was too far behind Caleb's head for his eyeline to reach.

He held his breath, willing himself not to pant, or groan, or worse yet, *cry* in front of this pretty young woman.

She glanced down at him, startled a little at the sight of his open eyes, then seemed to regain her composure before speaking.

"It's okay, Mr. Patton. Your pain meds have just run empty. I'll be right back with more for you. You just wait right here now, alright?"

She was gone before he could form a response, gone before he could wonder how he could possibly do anything *but* wait.

The minutes that passed before she returned with the thick plastic bag of medication, changed out the connection on his IV, and started the sweet numbing nectar flowing through his veins seemed impossibly long. Caleb drifted, lost on waves of pain pushing him in and out of consciousness, until the drugs took effect.

His body relaxed, and his mind was finally able to begin to process.

He took in the shape of himself beneath the blanket. The bulkiness of it all.

Casts, he thought. *I'm broken.*

He tried to look all the way down to his toes, but something was in the way. No matter how he tilted his eyes or his head, a line of gauzy whiteness obscured the bottom edge of his vision. As his brain came fully online, as the pieces of the horrible puzzle came together, two troubling realizations dawned on him.

The gauzy whiteness was just that: gauze.

His entire head seemed to be wrapped in it.

Not just his head.

His *face*.

What was wrong with his face?

And an equally pressing question: where was Colton?

The funeral was too massive for any church or funeral chapel to hold. Colton Patton, one half of the Golden Boys of Gideon, was eulogized, memorialized, and grieved in the only place that could hold the hundreds of people in attendance, a place strangely fitting, considering whose broken and battered body lay in the navy-blue casket in the center of it all.

It was the first, and the last, funeral ever held in the high school football stadium.

Caleb was pushed in, slumped in a wheelchair, his veins pulsing with the finest of painkillers, broken bones mending within the hard cocoon of his casts, face wrapped in fresh bandages, a sight inspiring pity in the hearts of all who saw him.

The seats were filled with people of all ages; classmates, teachers, family, friends. The day was warm and Caleb could feel the beads of sweat that rolled down the wrinkled flesh inside his casts. He barely heard the words spoken about his brother, his mind blank and drifting. He felt like a ghost, a hazy bit of mist floating above the stadium.

And then it was over, and he was being lifted carefully into the ambulance that would take him back to his room.

He wanted to go home, wanted to be away from the sterile feel and antiseptic smells of the hospital, away from the constant beeping and the conversations just beyond his door.

And yet a part of him did not want to go home. A part of him dreaded it. Dreaded that moment when he would walk – or rather, be wheeled – into the room he had shared with his brother, his twin, his other half, for eighteen years.

A room that would now belong to him alone.

But the hospital would be his home for a while longer. Every day his face needed fresh bandages, ointment, careful inspection by doctors who barely hid their true feelings behind plastered-on smiles.

Caleb's body, he found out, had been thrown from the car as it tumbled down the embankment. He hadn't worn his seatbelt, and ultimately, this was what had saved him. Colton, strapped in, had remained trapped in the car, hitting every tree and boulder on the way down before finally coming to a stop, upside down, two hundred feet below the road above.

Caleb's life had been saved when his body went headfirst through the windshield, his face taking the impact of the shattering glass.

He did not know what he looked like now. He had not seen it, had not held a mirror to his bandaged features, had certainly not dared to look at what lay beneath the wrappings.

In his mind, he pictured his reflection, his skin cut with a hundred tiny red nicks. Perhaps a cool scar beneath one eye.

Wishful thinking.

On the day the doctors proclaimed they were ready to remove the bandages for good, this illusion was shattered completely.

The pretty young nurse was in the room, standing patiently behind the doctor as he slowly unwrapped the gauze. The look in her eyes was not one Caleb was used to seeing when girls looked at him. There was a quick flash of fear, followed by a wave of revulsion, her countenance arranging itself finally into a look of pity.

It was the pity that hurt the most.

Caleb was sent home soon after.

He still had not looked in a mirror.

He knew that what he would see there had every chance of severing the tenuous grasp he still had on any kind of sanity, any kind of hope for the future.

He also knew he would have to face himself eventually, and so, on that morning when he woke in his own bed for the first time in eight weeks, he steeled himself for what was about to come, gritted his teeth, forced his stiff limbs into submission, sat up in bed, and picked up the mirror which had lain there on the bedside table, taunting him, through all the long hours of the night.

He kept his eyes closed at first, holding the mirror in front of him, taking deep breaths to center himself and prepare for what he was about to see.

Caleb opened his eyes.

There was… nothing wrong with his face at all.

He looked exactly as he always had.

Except… wait…

That small mole, just beneath the left eye.

That wasn't his.

That wasn't *him.*

Caleb Patton stared into his brother's eyes.

His chest hitched, up and down, short, anxious breaths making audible sounds in the quiet room.

He opened his mouth.

The reflection which looked back at him did not follow suit.

And yet...

A blurry outline, behind this strange reflection – behind his brother's face – *did* move, did open its mouth.

Caleb brought the mirror closer, peered into it, and as he watched, his brother's perfect skin and smile faded, and the thing which had been behind it came forward. Caleb found himself looking at his true reflection, his face a lumpy conglomeration of scar tissue, purple lines crisscrossing the once-smooth skin, his lips pulled out of shape, his eyes hidden deep within the swollen tissue that surrounded them.

His whole body shook; the mirror dropped to the bed and slid off to the floor below. Caleb's mind went blank, retreating from the truth of what he had seen, what he was, what he had become.

A monster.

The following months were not kind to Caleb Patton. Though his body healed enough – slowly – to function at the most basic level, it quickly became apparent to him, and everyone else, that he would never truly be himself again. He would never run early morning laps around the park, never climb the boulders out at Highline, never score another winning touchdown.

He could barely stand upright, could barely walk across a room. He could not even do those without pain that sometimes took his breath away.

And he couldn't bear to look in the mirror for more than a moment. Always, always his brother's face looked back at him, and the longer he looked at it, the more Colton's easy smile turned into an angry scowl, a rage-filled grimace, a look of pain and frustration and blame that made Caleb's stomach churn with guilt.

Why was he still alive when his brother wasn't?

And who was truly the lucky one?

Caleb's mind swung back and forth between a feeling of remorse and shame and one of anger that he was the one left behind. In his darkest moments, he hated his brother for taking the easy way out. Why was *he* the one still here, still living in this now far-from-golden world? Why was *he* the one doomed to a lifetime of pain and discomfort and loneliness? Why was *he* the one left behind with this hideous, monstrous face, while the world would remember Colton in all of his perfect, beautiful glory for the rest of time?

The idea filled Caleb with such fury and resentment that he smashed every mirror in the house.

Above the bathroom sinks. Sitting atop the bedroom dressers. Even the mirror that hung in the hall beside the front door.

Every one, smashed.

Caleb's knuckles split, sliced by the breaking glass, rivulets of blood falling from his hand to the floor as he walked, a trail of sanguine suffering which led his parents, when they returned home, to the hall bathroom, where Caleb sat slumped in the corner, dripping red onto the thirsty fibers of the bathmat.

The broken mirrors were removed from the house, the shattered glass swept up and bagged, carried carefully out to the bins at the side of the garage.

It wasn't enough.

Every reflective surface showed him the same thing.

In the side of the toaster, in the nighttime opaqueness of the patio doors. In the curvature of his mother's brass lamps, in the blank screen of his laptop, in every puddle.

In the great glass windows of every store he hobbled past, the same image greeted him: his own ruined body and grotesque face, and there with it, superimposed over his own reflection or standing smugly alongside it, the perfect form of his dead brother.

Caleb grew increasingly angry. Increasingly resentful. Grief and guilt transformed into wrath and rage, panic and paranoia.

Everyone – his parents, his friends, the police, the whole town – tried to give him understanding and acceptance. Many blind eyes were turned to his increasingly erratic and violent behavior. His parents' bank account dwindled as they paid one shopkeeper after another for repairs to their cracked, smashed, broken windows.

But the day came when people could no longer look the other way, no longer look on him with pity and tenderness. A day when grace and mercy turned away, replaced with something cold and hard.

The day Caleb put his fist through the front window of the Gideon Diner, the flying shards of glass scoring cuts into the tender flesh of little Emily Vaughn, who was just trying to enjoy a chocolate milkshake with her parents after the first day of third grade… that was the day the town decided it had put up with enough.

Stonehearst Psychiatric Hospital, just a few miles outside of town, was a modern sort of facility, all gleaming glass and stainless steel.

Caleb Patton had to be blindfolded just to get him through the doors, down the endless, labyrinthine hallways, and into his own special patient room, one in which every surface which might possibly cast even the haziest reflection had been removed.

He sat with doctors in that room, with nurses, with specialists, with every sort of head-shrinking expert the county could attract. Many diagnoses passed the lips of these most intellectual of men and women. Many pills passed the lips of their patient.

But no matter the treatment, no matter how high the hopes, every single time a mirrored surface was brought into Caleb's proximity, he would see

his own ruined visage

and his brother's grin – was it joking or malicious? he couldn't tell –

and the calmness of Caleb's mind would break, the great wave of guilt and sorrow and self-pity and *rage* rising and crashing over him, overwhelming him, sweeping him away in a tide of red fury until all faded once more to black.

Thus ten years passed. Ten years in which Caleb Patton, once one half of the Golden Boys of Gideon, grew hunched and weak, anxious and reclusive, a strange sort of modern monk in a windowless cell.

Until today. Today was going to be different.

Caleb had counted down, marking off square after square on the calendar taped to his wall.

May twentieth.

Ten years exactly since that fateful night.

And Caleb had plans to celebrate.

Marie came in just after the clock mounted high on the wall – digital, no round glass that might reflect the slightest hint of the room – clicked over to nine o'clock.

She was Caleb's favorite nurse, one of the few who had never once reacted in any way, good or bad, to the sight of him. He appreciated this.

She was cheerful, but not annoyingly so. She was efficient. She was practically the only person in the facility who would interact with him, taking on the role of nurse and aide and housekeeper all in one.

She bustled in that morning with her usual smile. In one hand she held a glass of water, in the other a small plastic cup of pills. A pile of fresh white towels was tucked beneath one arm.

Her key card was attached to her belt with a pink plastic clip.

Caleb smiled.

In his mind's eye, Colton leered.

Caleb swallowed the pills.

He'd become an expert at vomiting them back up as soon as she left.

He waited patiently and quietly while she stacked the clean towels in his bathroom and gathered up dirty laundry.

A quick, practiced movement of his hand, and a pink plastic clip disappeared into his pocket just as she turned around.

The moment the door clicked closed behind the nurse, Caleb rushed for the bathroom. Two fingers went down the back of his throat, pressing firmly against that sweet spot that was sure to bring up the medication, swimming in yellow bile.

He was out of his room, down the hall, and swiping his way out the heavy exit door at the end of the corridor within minutes. He knew where that door led; he had seen the nurses and aides slip out onto the roof of the walkway that connected this building with its neighbor a thousand times, secret stolen moments with the sweet release of a cigarette or joint.

Caleb's slippers made quiet crunching noises as he passed along the gravel-topped roof. His arms and legs ached, stiff with old injuries and disuse, as he climbed the ladder to the next level up on the roof of the adjoining building. He scurried, as quick as his protesting muscles would allow, from one rooftop to the next, until at last he had reached the furthest building of the complex.

The drop was less painful than he'd anticipated, though it did knock the breath from his lungs for a moment. The thought flitted through his mind that perhaps he *was* hurt, that perhaps the immense rush of adrenaline speeding along his veins kept him from feeling the pain that the fall should have caused. No matter. He would put his body through plenty more before the day was over, and any pain accumulated in his bones and muscles and sinews would be gone by nightfall.

Gone for good.

He allowed himself a small chuckle. The alarms were conspicuously silent; they hadn't even noticed he was gone yet.

The stretch of woods that shielded the walls of Stonehearst from the town of Gideon – or was it shielding the town from the hospital? – was no match for Caleb Patton. A childhood of running and climbing through the surrounding forest had made the dark, shady spaces between the trees a comfortable means of escape. The fresh air rushing over him as he jogged between the massive trunks and ducked beneath the stretching branches gave Caleb a buzz like he hadn't felt in years.

The morning sun rose steadily in the sky as he made his way across the miles between the place he had run from and the place he was running to. Caleb's slippers were not made for this kind of travel – he had to shuffle more than run – but within a couple of hours, the trees began to thin. The ground beneath his feet took on a gradual downward slope, and Caleb could see the tops of the buildings along Main Street in the valley below.

He paused near the edge of the forest, keeping to the shifting shadows of the treeline. He lowered himself to the ground and rested, letting his heart rate slow and his tired muscles gain back some of their strength, as he watched cars cruise along the road and people walk the sidewalks, ducking in and out of shops and restaurants.

A distant rumble made him glance upward; off to the west, dark clouds stretched across the horizon of an otherwise pleasant sky. A few minutes later, the wind picked up, drying the cooling sweat on Caleb's skin and pushing last autumn's leaves across the forest floor in a skittering rush.

Within ten minutes, the sun had disappeared behind the storm clouds. Beneath his sheltering canopy, Caleb saw the first drops fall before he felt them. A finger of blue-white lightning flashed from the sky, striking somewhere just north of town. The storm was moving fast.

He would need to move fast, too.

Caleb stood, took a moment to steady himself, left the protection of the forest, and started off down the hill.

Main Street had not changed much in the decade since Caleb had seen it last. The same uneven sidewalk, the same painted-over bricks, the same rush of cold air into the hot outdoors whenever someone entered or exited a building.

The looks people gave him had not changed, either.

He could see it in their eyes, see the thoughts and emotions as they passed across their faces: confusion, concern, fear.

Caleb looked around for something heavy. In a display outside the antique shop, he saw what he wanted. An antique ashtray stand, roughly two-and-a-half feet tall and made of solid cast iron, seemed to call to him. He picked it up, ignoring the alarmed looks of the people who passed him on the sidewalk as he hefted the weapon's weight in his hands. He nodded; this would do nicely indeed.

He stepped in front of the store's front window. Within, a cluttered display of vintage signs and pottery sat gathering dust. But between, in that place that he now understood as a world all its own, in that thin dark space where reflections lived, waiting and watching, Caleb looked at himself.

And his brother.

Colton's tall, muscular form stepped forward, eclipsing the image of Caleb's own twisted body. He bounced back and forth on the balls of his feet, an athlete ready to perform, a runner ready to start a race, a fighter ready to knock out his opponent in one strong, swinging punch.

Caleb's scarred face pulled into a sneer.

Hello, there, brother.

So nice to see you again.

Been having fun all this time while I rotted away in that room?

Been enjoying your freedom?

Colton's head tilted back in a laugh. Caleb could hear it, echoing inside his own mind, reverberating against the inside of his skull, mocking him.

He swung the ashtray stand. It hit the window of Giddy Gideon's Antique Shop with a strangely deep crash, the sound that of the demolition of something far more solid and weighty than a single pane of glass.

The people nearby shrieked and jumped back in surprise. An indignant cry rose from inside the shop, but Caleb did not care. He had moved on.

All along the length of Main he stalked, stopping at each window, his own reflection showing stark against the storm-darkened sky, his brother's image superimposed, perfect and evil, beautiful and cruel. One by one, Caleb smashed the windows, the doors, any surface diabolical enough to show him his own ruined countenance next to Colton's flawless image.

A swing of his arms.

Take that, you son of a bitch – sorry, Mom.

The stand raised high over his head.

How dare you stand there and pity me?

Footsteps stalking the glass-littered sidewalk from one storefront to the next.

You and your perfect, fucking face.

The stand positioned over his shoulder like a baseball bat.

Why, Colton? Why? Why me? Why would you leave me here? Like THIS?

Screams and shouts from the townspeople as bitter tears ran down his misshapen face.

Look at me, Colton! Look at me, a monster, while you remain forever perfect.

The loud and glorious sound of shattering glass.

Look at me when I talk to you! Look at me, you coward!

The distant wail of sirens.

It's not fair! It's not fair! It's not fair! It's... not...

A shard of glass, one that fit perfectly in his hand, its deadly point flashing in the light from the store just behind him.

I see you there, Colton. I see you hiding.

Half of his brother's face visible in the shard, one cool, condescending eye staring up at him as he stumbled off the sidewalk and into the center of the street.

Time to come out, Colton. I've suffered long enough. Your turn.

The people giving him a wide berth, foot traffic stopped twenty feet back in either direction, a blank space in a crowded street reserved for his final act.

Do you see the way they look at me, brother? Do you see the horror and disgust on their faces? No more! Let's trade places. I'll go in there; you come out here.

The ashtray stand long abandoned. The glass shard held carefully in two hands, raised like an offering to heaven, the blood of Caleb's sacrifice trickling down both arms.

Time to come, out, brother.

A flash of brilliant lightning as the once-strong arms found their final strength, plunging the blade of glass in a perfect downward arc.

The glass covered quickly in blood as it found its home deep in Caleb Patton's neck.

Caleb dropped to the ground, his knees giving out and his body folding beneath him like a rag doll. His eyes grew wide for a moment. The rain was warm, welcome on his quickly-cooling skin.

Two EMTs came rushing toward him and knelt down, dropping their bags beside them. Caleb did not have the strength to resist the men's ministrations. All he could do was gaze upward as the feel of hands on his body grew more and more distant.

"Hey, hey, buddy, stay with me, okay?"

Caleb's pupils shrunk, pulling him away from that blissful oblivion he had just been drifting in. His eyes focused for one brief moment on the man kneeling above him.

On the man's dripping hair, the frantic expression in his eyes.

On his glasses, on the drops of water like pinprick stars on a black background, and...

And...

The reflection of his brother's face, his brother's eyes.

His brother's eyes, filled with...

With sorrow.

With grief.

A flicker of confusion twitched across Caleb's scarred skin.

Colton—

No sound came from Caleb's throat, but he lifted a hand, his fingers brushing against the EMT's glasses for the briefest of seconds before his arm dropped, his head fell to the side, and finally, finally... he saw nothing at all.

DOUBTS

The house smelled of flowers. A heady, overwhelming fragrance; perfume mixed with stagnating water, underscored with the slightest hint of decay. Ben's head swam with the scent. His eyes seemed to pulse with the beating of his heart, the pain in his head like bone scraping over concrete.

The rooms were the same and yet not. The furniture sat in the same places it had sat for years, the pictures hung in the same places on the walls, yet everything seemed skewed, tilted, off in the most barely-noticeable ways, like an image caught in the corner of your eye that, when you turn toward it, is gone.

The heater kicked on as it was meant to do. Warm air hummed through the vents, stirring up the headache-inducing, eye-watering odor of flowers all over again.

Ben could taste it – *taste* the smell – in the back of his throat with every inhale. He sat on the sofa, forcing himself to take deep breaths, in through the nose, out through the mouth, while his hands clenched into fists over and over again.

Down the hall, Nora made a sound in her sleep – the kind of soft, bittersweet sigh that only small children can make.

Ben tensed. He looked toward the bedrooms with bloodshot eyes. He felt like he'd been crying for days, long hours of sobbing and even longer hours trying to hold it together so he didn't look like a blubbering fool in front of everyone else. God, his eyes hurt. His head hurt. His whole body hurt.

His heart. His heart hurt most of all.

He waited a few moments, breath held, to see if Nora would wake up. He pictured her turning over in her bed, blonde curls spread across the pillow, settling down into a more comfortable position, drifting back into the blissful slumber of childhood.

The poor girl. She'd been through a lot these last few days, too. He had to remember that. Had to remember that not only had he lost his wife, his best friend, the love of his life, but Nora had lost her mother as well. It was clear the child hadn't really grasped the situation yet; perhaps she couldn't. It seemed as if Nora were simply waiting for Mommy to come home, unable to comprehend a world in which Mommy never came home again.

"Oh, God, Sam, I can't do this." He spoke the words to the empty room, to the unresponsive air. Then Ben Garrett lay his head against the armrest, pulled the old quilt from the back of the couch, and willed himself to think of nothing at all, pushing all thoughts away as they came, until a drifting black numbness cradled him in its embrace and carried him away.

"Daddy!"

Ben jerked awake, confused and panicked for a moment at the weight on his chest. As his brain fought its way up from the murky depths of sleep into consciousness, he recognized the feeling: Nora had climbed onto the sofa and attached herself to him, her chubby arms wrapped around his neck and her head resting warm against his sternum.

Little spider monkey. He chuckled at the thought, his mind for the briefest moment living only in the present, before the horrible truth of the past flooded in. A sob rose in his throat; he swallowed it down, the taste like bitterness and dust.

Ben sat up, Nora still firmly attached, her fingers lacing together tightly behind his head. He patted her back a few times, ran his fingers through her tangled curls. "Good morning, sweetheart," he said, his voice hoarse.

Nora leaned back and looked up at him with a concern in her expression that both broke his heart and made him want to laugh. She unlaced her fingers and put a hand to his forehead, her eyebrows furrowed and lips pursed.

"You okay, Daddy? You sick?"

Ben took her hand, pressed it to his cheek, then kissed it. "Daddy's okay, sweetie. I'm not sick. Just tired."

Nora's big blue eyes narrowed into an expression of skepticism so like her mother's that Ben felt his heart shatter all over again.

"Come on, Nora, let's get you ready for school."

School was not really school, of course. Nora had only recently turned three, but Sam had felt it important that she attend a preschool of some sort, more for the social interaction than anything. Nora had been attending "school" for two months now, and Ben was happy to see that she loved going, loved playing with the other children.

Samantha had been happy, too. She was a good mother, a great mother, an excellent mother, but three years at home all day with no one but a toddler for company had frayed her nerves a bit, made her miss the world of adults, of work that was actually recognized in some way. So, once they were sure that Nora was happy in her "classes," Sam had found a job.

Her position was a hybrid role – three days each week, she worked from home, only going into the office on Mondays and Fridays for meetings and collaborative work.

Ben could tell she was happier. She thrived in this new stage of life, loved the routine of it. Fridays, she had said, were her favorite days. She got up, dressed in real-world adult clothes, drove to the office, spent the day showing off her work, sharing skills and knowledge, and then, when she was sick of other people, when her feet were aching and she missed her baby, she drove home, stopping at the grocery store for the makings of dinner, knowing that at the same time, Ben was picking Nora up from school.

Then they all came back together at home, making dinner while jazz played in the background, sharing stories from their day, enjoying their time together, made all the more precious for the time they had spent apart.

Except for last Friday.

Ben had picked Nora up and driven home to wait. And wait. And wait. But Sam never came. She never bustled through the door from the garage into the kitchen, arms full of grocery bags, kicking off her shoes and smiling that beautiful smile of hers.

Ben had called, texted, all to no avail. No answer. No explanation. Eventually, he had made Nora a dinner of mac and cheese and dino nuggets, a dinner Sam would have laughed at, had she been there.

He paced the kitchen, growing more and more agitated, as Nora sat at the counter, spooning cheesy pasta into her mouth and watching cartoons on the iPad – another allowance that Sam would surely have raised an eyebrow at.

Eventually, Ben had grown frantic and worried enough to start calling around to anyone who might know where Sam was. Her office phone went to voicemail. None of her friends had seen her. He was just about to start calling hospitals when the knock came.

A horrible, sinking feeling had invaded Ben's gut as he walked toward the door, a sense of awful foreboding, a dark, blank acceptance of news he had not yet heard but felt suddenly was inevitable.

Things were a blur after that. Cops. Neighbors. The site of the accident. The morgue. The funeral home. The cemetery. And all those god-awful flowers with their sickening fragrance.

Ben managed to get Nora to her classroom door in a reasonably decent state, though her socks didn't match and her curls were already falling loose from the messy ponytail he had hastily inflicted on her. Sam would have done a much better job, he knew that. Sam would have delivered their daughter to the teacher smiling, clean, coordinated, and adorable.

Ben returned home as the sky let loose a pathetic drizzling rain. Though it wasn't a home now, not anymore; it felt empty, a shell, a happy moment left too long on pause, so that its edges had begun to blur and lines of fuzzy static to stretch from room to room. The moment he opened the front door, the smell hit him anew, burning his sinuses and making him gag.

He pulled the box of giant trash bags from the shelf and in a quiet fury proceeded around the house, dumping flowers – vases, water, wilting blooms and all – into the bags. He stared at the trash bins for a moment before throwing the bags in the back of his truck and hauling them to the big dumpsters at the park a few blocks over. Was that even legal? He didn't know or care.

As he backed the truck up and turned it toward home once more, a sight in the sky caught his eye. A rainbow. A goddamn rainbow. Nora would have loved it. Sam would have, too.

With his truck idling in the parking lot, Ben's mind filled with the image of Sam sitting on the floor next to Nora's toddler bed, one hand smoothing their daughter's hair back gently from her face as she sang to her, the song that Sam's own mother had sung to her years before:

"Somewhere Over the Rainbow."

He could hear Sam's voice, quiet, soothing, a lullaby sure to guide even the crankiest child into peaceful slumber.

Ben put his head down on the steering wheel and wept.

The days passed slowly. Sunlight tracked across the walls; the picture on the muted television changed from soap operas to talk shows to the evening news to late-night infomercials, then circled back around and started all over again.

Ben's mind could not focus on any one thing. He washed the few dishes in the kitchen sink and left the murky water to stagnate. He bagged up the bathroom trash and forgot the bag next to the back door. The laundry started its third cycle through the dryer; the Dyson sat, upright, plugged in, between the vacuumed living room and the unvacuumed office.

How had she done it? How had Sam always managed to keep the household running, to keep everything clean and organized and lovely and welcoming, to keep the kitchen cabinets stocked and meals on the table, to keep Nora happy and clean and entertained?

Ben's phone buzzed each afternoon at 4:45, a reminder to get back in the truck and go pick Nora up. He didn't remember setting the alarm. Had he? Had someone else done it for him? His brain was too fuzzy to work out an answer.

Nora was her usual cheerful self when he picked her up, though Ben could feel the sympathetic gazes of every teacher and fellow parent he passed in the hallways of the preschool building. He hated it, hated feeling so pathetic, so pitiful, so woefully unprepared to do any of this without his wife.

Friday came. Two weeks since the terrible news. They had a quiet evening at home – Ben abandoned the idea of cooking entirely and had a pizza delivered, and he put the television on the Disney channel.

Let *The Little Mermaid* entertain Nora for a while. It was better than whatever his awkward attempts might turn out to be.

He should have known better, should have known not to feed a three-year-old pizza... and soda... followed by ice cream. But he hadn't had the strength to say no nor the patience to deal with any resistance she might have offered had he done so.

Nora had been in bed, asleep, for an hour when he heard her cry out. Ben rushed to his daughter's room, and the smell of the vomit hit him long before he saw the mess.

Exhausted, he led Nora to the tub, cleaned her off, stripped the sheets and blankets, and tucked her in to a remade bed in clean pajamas. A hopeless resignation filled his heart as he bagged up the soiled bedding and hurled it out into the garage.

Sam would have had it pretreated, washed, dried, folded, and smelling of sunshine and lavender by morning. Ben just didn't have the willpower for that. He'd buy new sheets if he had to.

As he passed by his own bedroom, the bed he had shared with his wife seemed to glare at him accusingly. How could he sleep there without her? How could he do *anything* without her?

The same thoughts which had circled his brain for days now returned in full force. Ben retreated to the living room, to his new resting place on the sofa. He sat with his head in his hands, whispering a prayer to his dead wife.

"Sam. Sam." The words shook as they sighed out of him. "I don't know how to do this, Sam, I don't know how to do this without you. I need you. Nora needs you. How can I raise her without you, Sam? I'm just... I can't... I'm going to screw it all up, Sam. I can't..."

Early morning spread tendrils of light through the living room blinds. Ben sat up, the crick in his neck a testament to the painful position – half sitting, half lying – that he had fallen asleep in. He rotated his head back and forth a few times, rubbing the back of his neck with one hand.

Ben stood and walked back to Nora's room; she was still asleep, her left thumb resting on the pillow inches from her open mouth. Ben managed half a smile. She had only recently broken the habit of sucking her thumb when awake; he supposed that she still resorted to this act of self-soothing at times in her sleep.

He pulled the door closed part-way behind him and let her sleep. It was Saturday; no need to get ready for school.

Ben was restless. He had done nothing but sit and mope for a week now. He walked aimlessly through the house. There was nothing to do. Everything still sat in its proper place. Not enough time had passed for things to accumulate dust. His hands twitched at his sides. He needed something to do.

His eyes lifted to the world beyond the windows.

Yes. Spring had finally arrived, and with it, all its attendant yardwork.

Ben headed for the garage and the tools of masculine distraction that would keep his mind from the pain that permeated every part of his psyche.

The sun rose higher in the sky. Ben's Weed Eater buzzed as he made his way slowly along the edges of the sidewalk, the street, the driveway, the curb. A few other men in the neighborhood were out doing similar things; lawn mowers and hedge trimmers joined the buzzing chorus.

Ben lost himself in the mindless work. He swung the long neck of the trimmer back and forth, meticulously and methodically performing that task which men have carried out since time immemorial: the taming of the great outdoors.

His mind was wonderfully blank, the only thoughts which flitted through it innocuous, painless, easy. He had nearly finished the front yard and was contemplating going inside for a bottle of water before tackling the back when Sam's voice jolted through him.

He felt the force of the sound like a lightning-strike, a punch to the gut that made him drop the trimmer and double over in shocked pain. His name. She had said his name.

"Ben!" The sound came again, loud, fast, frantic.

Ben looked all around, the world spinning about him as his neighbors went about their weekend routines, oblivious to his panic.

"Ben!" Her voice rose in pitch, worried, scared, distraught.

He closed his eyes, made himself breathe. It was all in his head, it had to be.

"Ben! Nora! Help Nora!"

Ben's eyes flew open, an entirely new panic flooding over him in prickling waves. He bolted through the door, headed for Nora's room, but something made him turn his head at just the right time.

The refrigerator door stood open.

Two small, bare, perfect feet stuck out from behind it.

Ben turned as he ran, hurrying toward that open door, expecting the worst yet still unprepared for the sight that met his eyes.

He took the scene in, processing every part of it in milliseconds.

The open fridge. The bag of grapes on the floor, a few plump purple fruits spilled out in a circle around it. Nora, sitting, legs outstretched, framing the bag. Nora's face, her eyes wide and frightened, her lips tinged blue, her hands up at her neck, grasping, clawing.

The sound that came from her throat was a raw, garbled cry for help, no louder than the tiny bit of air that managed to squeak past the obstruction that was depriving his baby of oxygen.

Instinct took over, instinct fueled by fear and rage. Ben grabbed his daughter roughly, her body a limp rag doll in his arms.

He found the position his hands had learned long ago at the first aid class Sam had insisted they both take, found that spot just above Nora's tiny little belly button (an outie, just like her mother), formed his fingers into fists, and thrust upward.

Five times. Five thrusts. That's what they had learned.

One.

Two.

Three.

Four.

The grape, as big around as his thumb, shot out of Nora's mouth and landed a few feet away, sitting innocently on the kitchen floor as if it hadn't just nearly taken the one good thing he had left in his life from him.

Ben turned Nora around and held her against his chest. God. His baby.

When Ben went outdoors an hour later, he took Nora with him. It had been stupid of him to leave her alone in the house for so long, stupid to be outside when she was inside, stupid to not check on her. He was a terrible father, useless, unfit. If it hadn't been for...

For what? Exactly?

What had happened?

What *was* that?

A fresh batch of goosebumps spread across his arms and legs every time he allowed himself to think about it. It had been Sam's voice, he was sure of it, but was it really just his own subconscious brain recognizing that he hadn't checked on Nora in a while, and forcing him into action in the most dramatic way it could?

Or had it been...?

No. He couldn't think like that.

Only crazy people thought like that, and he could not be crazy. He had to hold it together. For Nora.

Ben kept his daughter in sight as he worked. She was happy to be out in the fresh air and sunlight, blissfully covering the back patio in enormous chalk-drawn scenes full of flowers and clouds and butterflies.

Her mother had always loved to be outside as well, walking barefoot through the dew-drenched grass every morning, hot or cold, rain or shine. Sometimes, in the winter, she would come inside with the soles of her feet nearly frost-bitten, and Ben would wrestle her warmest socks over her freezing skin, pull her feet into his lap, and massage them gently until the feeling returned.

"Daddy?" Nora's voice broke Ben from his reverie.

He looked up. Nora stood peering intently into the large wooden planter he had built for Sam last autumn. She and Nora had filled the box with soil and sprinkled seeds across the top, Nora patting them into the dirt with her plump little hands.

"Daddy, when will our flowers grow?"

Ben swallowed hard. He had no idea. Sam was the one with the green thumb; he just cut the grass. He didn't know if the seeds would grow at all. Was there something else he should do to make them grow? *Oh, Sam, we need you...*

"Soon, baby. I'm sure they'll grow soon."

Nora bent forward, her face inches from the rich loam. She poked a finger into the dirt, then pulled back, satisfied. "Yes, Daddy. These are baby flowers. They'll grow soon."

Ben breathed a sigh of relief at his daughter's innocent trust. He watched as she went back to her bucket of chalk. She made great, sweeping curved lines over the top of her previous drawing. Pink, purple, blue, yellow, green. Ben smiled; the colors weren't in the right order – she was only three, after all – but it was, unmistakably, a rainbow.

Beneath her breath, Nora mumbled a song, a tune that Mark found himself humming along with. It took him a moment to recognize what the song was.

"Somewhere Over the Rainbow."

The weekend passed. Ben was ashamed to admit that he was relieved to drop Nora off at school on Monday morning. He had one more week of bereavement leave, for which he was thankful. He didn't think he was quite ready to face his boss, his co-workers, his desk, his eight hours a day of paperwork.

Each day that week seemed much the same; Ben supposed they were falling into a new sort of routine. Up in the mornings, breakfast, getting Nora dressed and off to school. Picking her up in the afternoons, dinner, bath, bed. He knew he was hitting all the important parts but could not help feeling that his mind wasn't really in the game.

What he did during the daylight hours, between dropping Nora off and picking her up, was as mysterious to him as it was to anyone else. He simply… existed.

Ben dreaded the weekend. In part this was because he knew that he would have to return to work the following Monday. In part it was because he just didn't know what to *do* with his daughter for all that empty time.

On Saturday morning, Ben woke to Nora playing quietly in her room. He could hear her, just barely, from his spot on the living room sofa. She was speaking, low, quiet, content. It almost sounded like she was having a conversation with someone, but Ben knew better than to let his thoughts go down that rabbit hole. No, she was probably just playing with her dolls, making them talk to each other. That was all.

Nora emerged from her bedroom around nine, and Ben listened to her bare feet pad into the bathroom. God, he was glad Sam had gotten her potty-trained before… before all this. He had no idea how to go about such things.

The toilet flushed. Nora came down the hall, curls bouncing, the ruffled hems of her pajama pants three inches off the floor. She'd need new clothes soon. Something else Sam would normally have taken care of. God, was there anything *he* was actually capable of doing?

"Daddy," Nora said as she climbed into his lap. A statement, not a question.

She placed a hand on each of his cheeks and turned his face toward her, their noses almost touching.

"Daddy. Today we will go to the zoo."

Ben snorted a laugh. The seriousness on her little face was too much.

The zoo. It *was* a nice day. Ben almost convinced himself to say yes. But then he thought of all those people. All those happy families. All those *whole, complete* families. The husbands and wives holding hands as their children skipped along in front of them.

Then a thought flashed through his mind: what if Nora needed to go to the bathroom while they were there? He couldn't go into the women's room with her. He couldn't take her in the men's room with him. Could he? Surely not. Did he send her into the restroom all alone? Wait till a mom went in with her own kids and ask her to take Nora along? Try to find a zoo employee and ask them?

Helpless, hopeless panic washed over him.

"No, Nora, sweetie, I don't think so. Not today."

Ben's mind rushed along at a million miles a minute.

Nora jumped off his lap. She planted her feet on the floor and put her hands on her hips. Her eyes narrowed. "Yes! Daddy! We! Go! To! The! Zoo!"

Ben's heart pounded fast in his chest. The room spun. Or was he spinning? He was losing it, losing control, losing it all…

"No, sweetie, no, I'm sorry, but…"

Nora stomped her foot on the ground, a movement so ineffectual it would have been funny under different circumstances.

"I want Mommy! Mommy would go to the zoo!"

Ben felt the world tip sideways.

"Well, Mommy's not here!"

He heard the shout, heard the anger and the frustration and the sorrow in his own voice; he knew it was the wrong thing to do, the wrong words, the wrong tone, the wrong volume, but he could not stop it.

Nora scrunched up her face. Ben felt the wail coming before the sound ever left her mouth. One brief cry, then she seemed to pull all her sadness back inside herself, a secret pain she would not share with the daddy who had yelled at her.

Nora stood for a moment, tears streaming down her small cheeks, her whole body shaking, before she turned and ran to her bedroom, closing the door behind her so carefully and quietly that Ben wondered if she would ever forgive him.

The rest of the day passed in strained silence. Nora kept to her room. Ben mostly left her alone.

He was surprised, when he knocked gently at the door and then stepped inside to see if she wanted any lunch, to see that Nora had dressed herself, and even managed to push her unruly hair back from her face with a wide purple headband. She sat on her bed, surrounded by stuffed animals, a pile of picture books in front of her, the top one open to a colorful page.

She had accepted his offer of lunch, but had eaten in her room, by herself. Ben had stared at his own lunch for nearly an hour before scraping the sandwich into the trash.

Dinner was no better. Nora walked begrudgingly to the table and ate her spaghetti in silence. She washed her own face and hands with a damp washcloth afterward, then changed into pajamas and crawled into bed at exactly eight o'clock.

Ben knelt beside her and kissed her forehead. Tears slid down her cheeks when she squeezed her eyes shut.

"Good night, sweetheart," Ben whispered.

A moment passed. Nora kept her eyes closed tight.

Ben stood, defeated, and walked to the door.

Nora's small voice, when it came, was barely more than a sigh.

"Good night, Daddy."

Ben sat for a while on the sofa. Everything hurt. Everything was wrong. He was falling apart, losing it, failing. He had to pull himself together but he didn't know how, didn't know how to break out of this cycle of grief and longing and loneliness. He didn't know how to raise a little girl by himself, didn't know what to say or do when she was hurt or upset, didn't know how to play dolls or dress-up or tea party.

But he had to do *something*. Had to drag himself out of this rut he was in and back onto a path where things would be better.

He walked to the bedroom. Their bedroom, his and Sam's.

His bedroom now.

He stared at the bed. He lowered himself gently onto the edge of the mattress, careful not to disturb Sam's side and the faint impression of her body it still held.

Ben sat, unmoving. He did his best to remain stoic, firm, strong.

He fell onto the pillows, pulling Sam's against his face, breathing in the scent of her: shampoo, lotion, sweat from their last round of lovemaking, the faintest trace of her favorite citrusy perfume. He buried his face in the memory, holding the pillow for dear life, a physical object taking the place of his wife, wholly inadequate and yet the closest he would ever be to her again.

Ben cried, ugly sobs muffled in the feather-down, until he ran out of tears and the shuddering convulsions of his body slowed and stilled.

In the quiet, he heard it: the faint crackle of the baby monitor.

Sam had insisted they keep using it, arguing that even though Nora was no longer a baby, there was no harm in being able to hear her, in case she woke up sick or scared or needing them in some way. Ben had acquiesced; he was a deep sleeper anyway and the few sounds that came through the speaker were only so much more white noise to him.

He heard the sound that came over the monitor now.

He had thought Nora was asleep, but he could hear her, crying. Her sobs were a quieter, more tender, utterly more heartbreaking version of his own. A new pain cascaded through Ben's senses. Not the pain of losing his wife, but the sympathetic pain of a parent when their child is in need.

He stood up, intent on going to Nora's room to hold her, to comfort her, as he should have been doing for the last three weeks.

But a new sound stopped him.

Nora's sobs lessened to mere sniffles. He could hear the faint movement of her head against the pillow; he pictured her nodding as she murmured a quiet, "Mmm-hmm."

Then it came.

The song.

Sam's voice.

A mother singing a lullaby of rainbows and bluebirds and lemon drops to an upset child.

A lullaby sure to guide even the crankiest of children into a peaceful slumber.

The voice was quiet, distant, yet it seemed to fill the room, the house, Ben's soul with feelings he had not experienced in weeks: peace, and hope.

Ben checked on Nora ten minutes later. She slept, curled up on her side, peaceful. Ben stood in the center of her room for a moment, looking around, breathing, hoping...

There was a comfortable warmth to the air, a calm and embracing quiet, and just there, if he breathed in deeply enough, the slight but unmistakable fragrance of citrus perfume.

The next morning, Sunday, Ben woke up in his own bed, having slept well for the first time in nearly a month. He peeked in at Nora; she slept on her back, snoring quietly. Ben smiled and left her to it.

He straightened the house, started a load of laundry, opened all the blinds to let the light shine in. When Nora woke, he had French toast ready, with extra icing, and chocolate milk in frosty glasses.

Ben's skills at ponytail-making still needed work, but he had no doubt that he would get better, and until then, well, Nora didn't seem to mind the stray hairs that came loose and floated around her face.

After breakfast, they went out back to play. It only took Nora a minute or two to find the surprise: in the planter, dozens of green shoots, three inches tall, some with tiny purple buds beginning to form in their centers.

"Daddy! Daddy! Our flowers are growing! Daddy! Mommy said they would, and Mommy was right!"

Ben knelt beside the planter with his daughter, showing her how to touch the plants gently, telling her all the things he had heard Sam say: "Be gentle with them. Make sure they have sunshine and water. Keep them safe. Talk or sing to them – they like that. It's really not hard to make things grow; just think about the things you need and give those same things back. Love, and care, and attention. That's all."

"And food, Daddy. Things need food to grow."

Ben laughed, the first real laugh in longer than he cared to admit.

"Yes, Nora. Love and care and food."

"Our flowers are going to grow up big and beautiful, Daddy. Mommy helped me plant them, and you can help me take care of them and make sure they grow."

Ben looked up. There were tears in his eyes, but they were not tears of sadness. The faintest of rainbows stretched across the sky, disappearing halfway to the horizon. Ben could almost feel Sam's hand on his shoulder, hear her laughter, see the mischievous sparkle in her eyes. She was gone, but she was still with them, where it counted. He would raise Nora alone, yet not alone.

"Yes, sweetheart," he said, turning his attention back to his daughter, "take care of things and watch them grow. That's my job."

DESIRE

Resisting the urge to check had been easy enough at first. The thought had merely passed through her mind, a quick observation among other, more pressing, matters. It wasn't that she missed him, not exactly. It wasn't that the conversation would go anywhere. It was just that it had become so normal, so routine, for one of his messages to pop up every three or four months, and it seemed like it should be about time for another one.

Yet none came.

Miranda Bower went about her days as a housewife, keeping herself busy with laundry and vacuuming and grocery shopping. The boys were preparing to go back to school after the winter break – Brandon to his third year at state university and Jason just beginning his educational career as a freshman at the same. Their father – her husband, William – was bursting with pride that both of his boys were following in their old man's footsteps.

Miranda was just glad that for the next few months there would be less laundry and fewer dishes to wash. She loved her boys, but she craved a little peace and quiet, and a house that stayed clean for more than an hour.

Perhaps it was because her mental calendar truly realized that enough time had passed since his last message that there should be a new one, or perhaps because lately in her few moments of solitude her mind had drifted briefly back to that summer seven years ago. Whatever the reason, he was on her mind, and she began to be a little troubled by the lack of communication.

Maybe he'd finally moved on. Maybe he'd found someone he could have an actual, real-life relationship with, and he was now happy enough to not miss her, to not feel the need to reach out to her now and then as if making sure she at least still existed in the same world as him. Maybe she should just leave it alone.

It was easy to ignore the curious itch at first. And then it wasn't.

It wasn't that she wanted him back, no. Enough time had passed that she could clearly see that the guilty pleasure she had enjoyed with him for those few glorious months had ended up more guilt than pleasure.

Although the pleasure had been…

She sighed thinking about it.

Daniel Long had been her friend since high school, although many years had passed since those long-ago school days before they reconnected.

Miranda had never given him much thought, even in her teenage days. He was a friend, but barely. An acquaintance who made her laugh now and then, a barely remembered face on the periphery of her adolescent memories. A nerdy sort of hanger-on, always on the edge of the crowd. The class clown.

But Daniel Long had grown up. Then, as it had done for millions of former classmates the world over, social media had reconnected them: Miranda and Daniel.

There had been lots of catching up at first. Lots of reminiscing. Lots of *what are you up to these days* and *tell me about your family*.

And then a little flirting.

Miranda had been truly surprised when Daniel confessed that he'd had a crush on her back in high school. She'd never known. She admitted – to herself, not to him – that even if she had known, it would never have gone anywhere. He simply wasn't her type.

Not then, anyway.

All those years later, though, she found herself experiencing a strange and unexpected pull, an attraction that sat uneasy in her gut.

He wanted to know where she lived; an innocent enough question. Hesitant to give her address, she gave him the general area. A week later, he had rented office space two blocks away.

"Did you do that to be close to me?" she had asked, joking but also overcome with an unsettling combination of both fear and hope.

"I wouldn't say that," he had answered. "But it sure doesn't hurt."

Things happened quickly after that.

Talk had turned from flirting to sexting to scandalous photos.

Then he had invited her to visit him at his office. She had left the boys stationed in front of the TV in the den, video game controllers in hand, and gone out for a walk.

A walk that took her down sunny sidewalks, through the neighborhood park, and directly to the door of Daniel's building.

Miranda's heart pounded in her throat as she went in, the cool darkness of the building a stark contrast to the bright summer heat outside. His office was on the second floor; she had only to climb a steep staircase to reach it.

She paused for a moment at the bottom of the stairs, one hand on the wooden banister, caught in the exact moment between what she knew she *should* do and what some dangerous part of her mind *wanted* her to do.

The sunny, happy world beyond the door, the world where she wasn't lying to her husband or chancing the ruination of her reputation, lay in one direction.

A dark staircase, a mysterious secret space, and a man whose words made her heart flutter and her body flush lay in the other.

Miranda took a deep breath and put her foot on the first riser.

The loft space above revealed more of itself with each step she took. It was a large room, open, shadowy, and cool. The walls were exposed brick, the ceiling a mesh of crisscrossing pipes.

Daniel's desk sat at one end; a small conference area featuring a white couch and chair was set up at the other. In between, a short counter and sink that served as a kitchenette.

Daniel stood when she reached the top, the look of surprise on his face showing that he had doubted she'd go through with this even more than she had.

But she *had* gone through with it. She was here. With this man who was not her husband. Miranda's legs trembled.

He walked toward her then, reached for her, enclosed her in his arms before she had a chance to process what was happening. Without a word, without warning, his face was buried in her neck, his mouth kissing and nipping at the tender flesh there.

Miranda had pushed against him and stumbled away backward, toward the top of the stairs. A panicked voice in her head told her to run, to fly down those steps and out the door and back to the comfort and safety of her home, her family, her perfect, safe little world.

But another voice stopped her. Another voice spat venom on the concepts of comfort and safety and whisper-shouted that *oh, God, she was so tired and so alone and William hadn't touched her, hadn't so much as looked at her with any hint of passion in his eyes in years, and she was so, so lonely and so, so desperate.*

She had not turned and run. She had stayed. She had asked with shaking voice that Daniel please be patient, be gentle, go easy on her, go slow. He had agreed.

She had then paced circles around his loft, body burning with nervous energy, while he leaned back against his desk, arms crossed, and watched her.

When she finally made herself stop pacing, when she stood still and lifted her eyes to meet his, he had seen something within them that she could not find the words to say.

He had not been patient, or gentle, or slow. In a moment he was across the room, tilting her chin up so that he could kiss her, rough kisses that would leave her lips swollen for hours afterward.

In no time at all he had turned her around, bent over the back of the creamy-white sofa, her pants and panties around her knees, one of his hands wrapped in her hair, pulling it tight, the other between her legs, working her wetness until a crescendoing cry escaped from deep within her.

Miranda was panting and sore as she left his loft that afternoon, panties damp, mind numb, her whole body tingling with adrenaline and shame and desire.

And then she had gone back. She had gone back so many times.

Brandon and Jason were roughhousing upstairs; their laughing shouts and thunderous footsteps broke Miranda from her reverie.

She lifted a hand to her throat and took a few deep breaths. Her mind had wandered back to that first time in Daniel's loft, calling forth the long-buried memories with startling clarity. She shook her head, dislodging the thoughts, and went back to sweeping the kitchen floor.

That evening the thoughts returned. Something felt… not wrong, exactly, but strange, *off* in some way. She tried to remember exactly when he had last texted her but couldn't. So that night, when her husband was in the shower, Miranda pulled out her phone and scrolled back through months of texts until she found the last one from him. Five months ago. She was right. He had never gone this long before.

Miranda allowed herself to scroll up through his messages. It had been the same thing for seven years, the same thing since the day she broke it off and told him that she couldn't stand the guilt anymore.

Every few months her phone would *ping* and a message from him would appear. The conversation always started off innocently.

What's new in your world? How are your kids?

But eventually it always came back around to sex. Daniel would tell her how beautiful she looked in her last profile picture. Then he'd start talking about her bedroom eyes, or her pouty lips, or the perfection of her porcelain skin.

She'd stop him, every time. She'd say *this conversation is heading to a place it shouldn't be,* or *you're doing it again, Daniel,* or *time to sign off, because we're not doing this.*

And he would say okay and apologize, and then another three or four months would go by before she heard from him again, and the cycle would repeat.

She told herself this was all okay, told herself that allowing him to contact her now and then was completely innocent, because she always stopped him before the conversation could proceed into those places it had no business going.

She wasn't even friends with him on any of her social media anymore, didn't pay attention to his life, didn't show him hers, except for those little bits she gave away in their messages.

She told herself it was innocent, but deep down she knew better. She knew the way her heart skipped when his name showed up on her phone. She knew the way her body tingled when he made that first attempt to turn the conversation toward things sensual.

She knew that after she cut him off, told him no, after he left the chat, she would run herself a hot bath, and behind the bathroom's locked door she would slip a hand between her legs and bring herself to the kind of pleasure her husband had never been able to give her.

And now it had been five months.

Miranda lay awake that night in the darkness, William snoring softly beside her, and thought about this. Should she care? Should she drop it? Should she keep on with her unimpassioned yet steady life? Should *she*, for the very first time, be the one who reached out to *him*?

The next morning, she did something she had not done in years.

She opened Facebook, went to the search bar, and typed in Daniel's name.

What she saw shocked her, shook her, left her speechless and numb.

There had been no posts from Daniel himself in the last month, but there were updates from his sister.

Four weeks ago: *Everyone please pray, Daniel has a really bad case of Covid. I've never seen anyone this sick before.*

Three weeks ago: *Daniel has been admitted to the hospital. This Covid is really kicking his butt. All the prayers and good thoughts, please.*

Two weeks ago: *Daniel is in a coma. The outlook is not good. Keep the prayers coming.*

Three days ago: *It is with a heavy heart that I let all of my brother's friends know that Daniel passed away around three this morning. He never woke up from his coma. Thank you for all your prayers, funeral details will come soon.*

Miranda read the words, over and over. How could that be? Three days ago. How could a person just disappear so completely from the world? Of course, people she had known had died before, but they were always older people, or people on the very edges of her life.

Nothing like this.

Nothing like this punch in her gut, this lightheaded swaying, this feeling like all the air had been sucked from the room and her lungs no longer worked.

This unexpected, crushing grief.

Daniel had not been a major part of her life for years, but he was always there, always a thought of *maybe* or *someday* or *if life had turned out different.*

Now he was just... gone.

No, she told herself, straightening up and shutting away all the painful emotions that threatened to overwhelm her; no, she had no time for such silliness when there were things to be done.

The boys were leaving the next week for school and William was off on a business trip a few days after that. She had all that laundry and packing to do, on top of all the normal chores.

And she needed to go grocery shopping. And get the oil changed in the car. Yes, things to do. Too many things to do.

She could not waste time grieving this man who had barely been in her life anyway.

At least not yet.

Miranda spent the day in busy productivity, forcing the thoughts from her mind whenever the image of Daniel's face would flash before her eyes. After dinner, she ran a hot bath, but she could not bring herself to slip a hand down to that most intimate part.

Never again would she be able to pleasure herself with fantasies of him, no, not with fantasies of a dead man. But she did think about him, and sitting in the bath with her knees drawn to her chest and her wet hair hanging in a curtain around her face, she did allow herself to cry.

The tears did not last long, she would not allow it. They fell, silent, into the bathwater, for a few minutes at most before she steadied her breathing and chastised herself for this display of emotion.

She lay back in the warm water, soap bubbles congregating along the edges of her body, and though she did not fantasize, she did reminisce.

The bathwater had grown cold by the time Miranda pulled the plug and climbed out of the tub.

She had let her mind run through every memory she could dredge up of those three months together, and in that she had found the tiniest hint of closure.

As she toweled off and pulled on her nightgown, she made up her mind that she would delete the messages from her phone, erase all evidence that they had ever had those conversations, sent those pictures, or, years ago, set up those secret rendezvous.

Then a horrifying thought hit her. If she had those messages and the pictures they contained on *her* phone, then he might also still have them on his phone.

His phone, which would now be picked up and possibly looked through by, well, anyone. His ex-wife, his daughter, his sister – his sister! who she went to church with! – anyone, really.

Miranda felt a heavy dread drop like an anchor into her stomach.

She lay awake for a long time that night, fighting against the panic that threatened to rise up and overwhelm her. If anyone looked through his phone, if those messages were still there, her entire life would be over. Her reputation would be ruined. Her marriage would be destroyed.

And then, when she finally fell asleep, Miranda dreamed.

She was there with Daniel, in the loft. The edges of the room were nothing but shadows, a spreading infinity of darkness. He grabbed her roughly, held her so tightly she could not get away no matter how much she struggled.

Hello, honey. Now, be a good girl. You know how I like it.

She had calmed then, both mesmerized by those words and still trained, after all these years, to respond to them.

With his palm against her neck and his thumb and forefinger grasping her jaw hard enough to hurt, tilting it up until once again she found herself staring at the ceiling, Daniel began to trail kisses down her body, lips and tongue and teeth against her shivering skin.

His hand slid between her legs; she closed her eyes and let out a sigh which was both pleasure and despair, relief and surrender.

Her eyes flew open when the other voices appeared. Murmurs, whispers, shouts. With her head still held firmly back, she could only make out the tops of people's heads, a whole crowd now surrounding them, but she knew somehow that they were all pointing, laughing, judging. Her secret was out, she was exposed, and she could not get away from it.

Daniel's hand continued to work away between her legs, and the rising pressure mixed with her panicked fear until she found herself fighting her way up from the dream and out of a tangle of sheets, William sleeping peacefully beside her.

The next few days were a whirlwind of activity preparing the boys to go off to school and William to spend a week in Houston on business. Miranda kept herself busy as always, but constant in the back of her mind pulsed a tremulous fear that she was going to be found out at any moment.

The day came for the boys to drive back up to the university. There was much hugging and laughing and perhaps a tear or two in Miranda's eyes. Then she and William turned and walked back into a blessedly quiet house.

Miranda dared to hope that perhaps in the three nights – or even days – between the boys' departure and the day William left she might get a little alone time with her husband.

She made sure her legs were shaved smooth and her hair and make-up were done just-so every day. She wore her laciest nightgowns to bed.

William was buried in work, in preparations for his trip, and was asleep every night long before she was. He did not touch her once save for an occasional peck on the cheek.

Thus had been her life for far too many years.

And then he was gone.

Two weeks without either her husband or her sons; the imagined days stretched out long and glorious before her. Miranda spent the first day giving the house a thorough cleaning, knowing that once it was clean, it would stay clean for the next thirteen days because she certainly wouldn't be making a mess.

That night, her body aching with a satisfying tiredness, she ran a hot bath, even pouring in a couple capfuls of her favorite bubble bath. She left the bathroom door wide open, because – why not? Then she dropped her clothes to the floor and climbed in.

Her panic over what might have been on Daniel's phone had abated. It had been two weeks now; surely if anyone were going to find anything, they would have found it already.

She told herself she wasn't going to worry over it any longer. She had thirteen days of irresponsibility ahead of her, and she was going to relax and enjoy every minute of it.

Miranda lay back in the tub, sinking into its depths until the water touched her chin and nearly covered her tented knees. She let her mind drift, steering it gently away from thoughts of both Daniel and of William, and even away from thoughts of the boys.

This was her time.

After a few minutes, she had reached a state of mindless bliss, only wispy clouds of thought passing through the welcome emptiness in her head.

The bathroom door creaked.

Miranda's eyes flew open, darting to the doorway. The door looked the same as she had left it, though it might have moved an inch. She couldn't be sure. Miranda held perfectly still, listening. The only sound in the house was the slow fizzing of her bubble bath. After a moment, she let her eyes drift closed again. It was probably just the house shifting.

A few minutes passed before she heard it again, louder this time: a long, drawn-out creaking. She opened her eyes slowly, half afraid of what she might see once they were open.

The bathroom door, which had previously stood half-closed, was now completely open.

Miranda sat up quickly in the tub, wrapping her arms around herself, covering her naked breasts. Was *that* just the house shifting?

Was someone *in* the house?

She was struck with her complete vulnerability. She was a woman alone, exposed, defenseless. Her phone was in the bedroom. If an intruder were to suddenly appear in the doorway, she'd probably fall and break her neck just trying to get out of the tub.

She waited, and listened.

Nothing.

No sound, no movement.

When enough time had passed that her heart had slowed from triple time to merely double, Miranda quietly slid her arm through the water and pulled the plug. She stood as gently as she could, trying not to make the water slosh about and make noise.

Quickly but carefully, she pulled her robe around her and then tiptoed to her bedroom across the hall. She didn't have a weapon, though she supposed she could find something to act as a makeshift club of some sort, but she knew that she would feel much better if she just had her phone in hand.

Once she had the phone, she began a systematic search of the house, checking in every closet, under every bed, making sure each window was locked, closing each door behind her as she left a room.

Downstairs, she checked the locks on the front and back doors and even stuck her head out to make sure the garage door was firmly down.

She was alone in the house, locked safely in. There was not a single sign that anyone had been there except her. Yet she could not shake the prickling feeling that someone *was* there, that someone was nearby, watching her every move.

She went through the house three more times before she went to bed, checking the locks on windows and doors. When at last she climbed into bed, she kept her phone in her hand beneath the pillow, conspiracy theories about radiation be damned.

It took hours for her body to relax, for her mind to release from its state of constant wary vigilance. She pondered turning on the fan for a bit of white noise to help her sleep, but decided against it in case it covered the sound of someone breaking in.

Finally, just after two in the morning, a peaceful wave of oblivious slumber washed over her, and her exhausted mind and body drifted away.

A moment later, the shadows in the corner of the room shifted.

The next day, Miranda moved through the house slowly. Her mind felt fuzzy, unfocused. Several times she would catch something, the slightest movement in the corner of her eye, and would whip her head in that direction only to find nothing there but the kitchen window or the towels hanging on the bathroom rack or the pillows still sitting, perfectly plumped, on the living room sofa.

That afternoon, a strangely warm day for January – a sure sign that a cold front would be moving in soon – as she lay on the chaise lounge in the garden, a book sitting ignored beside her, a fragrance drifted around her which she recognized but could not place. It was familiar, intimate. She breathed it in, her eyes roaming lazily over the few flowers which still dared to bloom in the winter chill. None of those matched the scent which settled heavy around her.

She closed her eyes, taking deep breaths, trying to parse out the different notes of the perfume.

Miranda sat straight up on the chaise, knocking her book to the ground in her panic. She knew now what the fragrance was.

It was the smell of him.

Of Daniel.

As soon as she recognized it, the scent drifted away. Miranda trembled as she made her way back into the house, glancing nervously around her as she went. She slid the patio door closed, locked it.

She stood for a long time looking out over the back garden, her eyes searching every shadow and dark corner.

For a week the feeling of unsettledness remained, always in the back of her mind. Sometimes she could go for hours, distracted by some task, without remembering to look over her shoulder, without wondering if she were truly alone.

But then the sensation would come creeping back, that icy finger tiptoeing up the vertebrae of her spine, and a tension would spread throughout her body, gripping her mind with a quiet panic until she had checked the whole house – every window, door, lock – again.

But she knew, in the moments when she dared admit it to herself, that the thing which now haunted her would not be stopped by walls or doors, by wood or glass. She knew that no lock could keep him out.

On the eighth day of her husband's business trip, Miranda felt something she had not felt in years: the firm, insistent caress of her dead ex-lover.

It was late in the day, just as darkness descended fully on the world beyond the windows. Miranda had picked at her food before dumping most of it into the garbage. All day long she had felt something coming, felt a growing pressure within the walls of the house and within the confines of her mind.

Her body was tense with anxiety, her blood vibrating as it rushed quickly through her veins.

It was too early to go to bed but she could not force her mind to settle enough for any task. She checked the locks one last time before lying back on the couch, one arm thrown up over her eyes to block out the light.

It was barely noticeable at first: a creeping chill that reached its fingers out, surrounding her, sliding beneath her clothes and slithering along her skin.

Miranda shivered.

But not just from the cold.

There was something in the way the chill glided against her, something in its pressure, in the way it moved, in the intimacy of its touch, that was sensuous, thrilling.

Arousing.

Miranda lifted her arm away from her eyes, blinking against the sudden brightness as she looked around quickly, panicked, half-convinced there was a person – a man – standing close enough to touch her.

The room was empty, yet she knew it wasn't. The touch upon her skin continued, a freezing trail that fanned to life a blazing fire beneath the surface. The fragrance she'd noticed earlier in the garden filled the air, settling over her like a weight that pricked goosebumps along her flesh.

Honey.

The voice was a whisper, a brush of air; her heart leapt with recognition.

"Daniel?" Miranda barely dared to breathe the name, but the moment she did, the sensations increased, took clearer shape.

Unseen fingertips traced lines along her thighs, the fabric of her clothing no barrier. The shadows from the corners of the room pulled together above her into the vague outlines of broad shoulders, arms reaching for her. The hovering darkness descended.

Miranda's throat constricted as the unmistakable form of a hand imprinted itself on the pale flesh there. She could feel the tension where his thumb and forefinger held tight to her jaw, pushing her chin up and back until her whole body arched, dangerously wanton, under the pressure.

When she felt the frosty tip of an ethereal tongue dart across her skin, Miranda released a moan which echoed through the empty house.

Her eyes fluttered and then closed, and in her mind, Daniel was there in the room with her, not a hovering spirit but a flesh-and-blood man. His hands were insistent, his mouth even more so.

Her body was lifted, moved, manhandled. Every movement was hard and rough, violent, and Miranda sighed and gasped at the glorious pleasure of the pain.

When Miranda woke the next morning, curled into a ball on the couch, still fully clothed, she thought for a brief moment that perhaps it had all been a bizarre but pleasurable dream.

The moment she moved she knew that was wrong. Every part of her body ached. A deep pain throbbed between her legs as she sat up. Her mouth was dry, her head pounding.

Water. She needed water.

Her muscles cramped as she forced herself to her feet and stumbled into the kitchen. Miranda filled a glass with water, gulped it down, and filled it again. Sipping more slowly this time, she made her way up the stairs and into the bathroom, each step sending a spike of pain deep inside her, the throbbing emptiness a grievous reminder of that which she craved.

She took her clothes off slowly, avoiding the mirror for as long as possible, afraid of what she'd see. When she did finally allow her eyes to turn to her reflection, she winced at what was shown there.

Bruises along her thighs. Handprints on her hips. The marks of fingers along her neck. Miranda ran a hand gingerly between her legs, unsurprised at the wetness she found there. At least there was no blood.

Yet.

She stood beneath the shower for a long time, letting the hot water soak through to the chill that had settled deep in her bones.

She swayed beneath the spray, tired and weak, willing herself not to think too deeply about the events of the previous night.

Her mind was not quite ready to face the truth of all that.

The day proceeded slowly, quietly. Miranda felt as if her every movement were underwater, the air around her just thicker than it should be, viscous, resistant, requiring too much effort.

She went through the motions of the day, rote routines: clean clothes, hair brushed, lunch. She took the trash out, walking barefoot across the freshly fallen snow without registering the cold on the soles of her feet, oblivious.

She washed the few dirty dishes, standing at the sink and staring out the window, the wet rag in her hand making circle after circle across the plate she held, over and over until the dishwater had gone cold and all the suds had vanished.

By the time the five o'clock news came on and the weatherman was busy predicting twelve to fourteen inches of snow, Miranda had half convinced herself that it had in fact all been a dream.

Maybe, in her grief – grief which she had pushed down and kept locked inside a soundproof cage – her subconscious had called forth exceptionally vivid dreams.

Maybe her body was bruised and sore simply because she had thrashed about on the narrow couch in her sleep. Maybe she had been so immersed in the scenes in her head that she had slipped her own fingers deep inside herself and made herself sore.

She stood and walked to the mirror which hung in the entry hall. The marks of fingers stood out clearly, unmistakably, vivid against her pale skin. She crossed her arms, tried to fit her own fingers into the prints. Her hands looked small and frail against the impossibly large bruises.

There was no way she had done that to herself, and she knew it.

It had been Daniel. Somehow, some way, he had come back to her. But why? Their fling had only been a few months.

Oh. But, what if...

Miranda stopped, frozen in front of the mirror, staring into her own troubled eyes, as a years-old memory washed over her.

Miranda was walking to Daniel's office. Her heart had not pounded this hard since the very first time she made this same journey. That time it had been an excited sort of nervousness. This time it was a terrified anxiety, a fear of both what Daniel would say when she gave him the news and of whether she would be strong enough to stand by her decision and tell him in the first place.

It was a hot day, mid-September. School had started a few weeks before; the park was nearly empty as she passed through it, just a few senior citizens out for their daily walks.

Miranda stood at the crosswalk, that same feeling of passing from one part of her life to another washing over her, rooting her to the spot. Three months earlier she had crossed from her safe little world into a new one full of excitement and new experiences. Now she was about to leave those new thrills behind and turn back to the mundanity of her secure, routine, mindless life.

And all because of William.

He had become suspicious. Miranda could feel it in the way he looked at her, the way his eyes lingered on her phone every time a message popped up.

He had started paying more attention to her in the bedroom, which should have been a good thing, but which only made her feel more guilty, because his advances were clumsy and weak compared to Daniel's confident expertise.

But deep in her heart, Miranda decided she loved him, and she would give him a chance. Maybe this new, more amorous side of him would eventually grow into something similar to what she had with Daniel, if she could just convince William to let go and have a little fun.

Plus, the guilt was eating her alive.

So here she was, standing at the crosswalk while the light changed over and over. A man on a bicycle went whizzing by, barely missing her, the wind in his wake whipping her hair back from her face. She realized then that there were tears in her eyes, and she wiped at them quickly, angrily.

She started across the street.

Daniel's building was, as always, dark and cool after the glaring sun and afternoon heat outside. It took a moment for Miranda's eyes to adjust. When she finally cleared the floating black spots from her vision, she glanced up. Daniel stood looking over the landing from the floor above.

A panic rose in Miranda's mind that nearly made her faint. This was too much. She couldn't do it, but she couldn't not do it, and the push-pull pressure of it all threatened to overwhelm her.

Daniel must have seen something in her expression, or perhaps he noticed her swaying slightly where she stood. He came loping gracefully down the steep stairs. The small entry area between the door and the stairs could barely hold them both at once. Their bodies were pressed close together in the tiny space.

Miranda's heart raced. Her mouth went dry. She closed her eyes against the spinning vertigo that threatened to pull her down.

"What's wrong, honey?" Daniel asked, his hands going to her arms, holding her steady.

Miranda couldn't speak. She opened her eyes and looked up at him, her mouth moving silently, shaking her head to try to convey what she needed him to understand: *no, no, no, no more.*

He pulled her closer, one hand sliding up into her hair. He was gentle, so gentle, a trait she had never known in him before. His sudden tenderness made the tears she had been holding back break loose and flow freely down her face.

Daniel looked at her, concerned, worry creasing the space between his eyebrows.

"Honey, what is it?" he asked, and Miranda noted the hint of panic that crept into his voice.

When she still didn't respond, Daniel leaned forward, closing the whisper of space that still lingered between them, and brought his lips to hers. The kiss was soft, delicate. Miranda let herself, for one moment, melt into it, let herself relax against him.

Then she pushed against him, pushed him away so hard that he stumbled against the bottom step. Confusion, then irritation, then the beginnings of anger flashed across his face as he stared at her.

The words rushed out of her, barely coherent mumblings, salty tears streaming into her mouth as she spoke. "I can't do this anymore, Daniel. It has to stop. I have to stop. I'm sorry. I can't do this. I have to go."

Miranda just had time to register the shock in his eyes before she turned and pushed against the door. She had taken one step out onto the sidewalk before Daniel's hand gripped her arm firmly, pulling her back. She looked up at him, and she knew that in her eyes he could see both her pain and her fear, her desire and her heartbreak.

She thought he was going to kiss her again. Part of her hoped he would try. But he didn't. He held her there, the inches of air between their bodies as solid a barrier as any brick wall. Daniel leaned down, and when he spoke his words took on a weight, a heavy certainty, sharp and piercing as a sword.

"You can go if you think you must, Miranda. I won't stop you. But you remember this, and you remember it until the day you die: you belong to me. I own you. You will always be mine. Always."

She stared, trembling, into his face for a second more before he released her arm. He walked away, back up the stairs, never turning back to look at her.

Miranda waited a moment, there in that liminal space between Daniel and the rest of her life, and she forced herself to make the decision that she knew was right, even though she wanted so badly to follow him, to beg him to forgive her, to love her, to let her stay there with him, forever.

She pushed through the door and walked away in the sunlight, the tears drying on her cheeks long before she reached her home, her husband, and her children.

I own you. You will always be mine. Always.

The words now raced in echoing circles inside Miranda's head as she stared at her own battered reflection.

Behind her, the room seemed to grow hazy, as though a fog were settling in, creeping across the rug and climbing slowly up the walls. The lights grew dim, their power draining as a new presence, a new power, took shape.

Miranda gasped, hands gripping the hall table she stood before, her eyes focused intently on the mirror, never leaving the swirling mist which now stalked slowly toward her in the shape of a man.

Daniel's voice whispered in her ear.

Honey.

His arms wrapped around her waist, his shadowy body pressing firm against her from behind. Miranda searched the place in the shadows where his eyes should be, but there was no face, no discernible features, only the vague outline of him, filled with that swirling darkness.

His hands lifted to her breasts, and once again her clothing presented no challenge to his ethereal touch. Miranda leaned back against the strangely solid feel of his insubstantial body.

Though she knew, in the logical part of her brain, that she was standing in her own entry hall fully clothed, she also knew, in the part of her which was only touch and sensation and fast-firing synapses, the part which was quickly overtaking her thinking, that she could feel Daniel's legs nudging her own thighs apart.

Could feel him pushing his way inside her.

Miranda moaned at first, cried out until she could no longer make any sound except the steady gasping of her breath as her body was shoved against the table again and again.

Eventually, even the heavy exhalations stopped. Her mind drifted to a place where there were no thoughts, where even the feel of Daniel's continuing thrusts were a distant sensation at best. She lay down across the table, her cheek pressed against the cool wood, and let the constant rocking lull her into a blissful state of uncaring oblivion.

She woke up on the cool tile of the entryway sometime later, her body collapsed where she had stood, every part of her thrumming with exquisite pain. Her hips were bruised both back and front, a sharp pain in the front where her bones had been ground for so long against the edge of the table and a duller pain behind where Daniel's hands had gripped her.

It took every ounce of determination she could muster to drag herself up the stairs and collapse into bed, still fully dressed but knowing without looking that beneath her clothing new bruises would be forming, turning from purple to green over the hours to come.

Miranda lost track of the days, of the hours. She stopped eating, barely drank enough to keep her exhausted body functioning.

Daniel came, again and again. He held her, used her. In every room of the house, at any moment of day or night. She was never safe. She felt his hands on every part of her body, his mouth kissing, sucking, biting.

It hurt like hell, left her bruised and battered and crying, and in those moments when she was lucid enough to think clearly, she had to admit to herself that she loved it, craved it, needed it; nothing in her life had ever made her feel more alive than when Daniel claimed her, stripped her of control, pushed her beyond the boundaries of all that was decent until all she cared about was his pleasure and the only word on her lips was his name.

He was killing her, and she welcomed that beautiful death, begged for it, with open arms.

Honey. His voice was in her head, even when she could not feel his presence. He whispered to her, all the things he would do to her, all the ways she would offer herself as sacrifice to him.

I own you. You will always be mine. Always. The words went round in her head until she wasn't sure if it was his voice or her own that repeated them.

Honey. Own. Mine. Always.

Honey. Own. Always.

Mine.

Always.

Always.

Always.

Always.

In the hours when Daniel wasn't touching her, Miranda crept from place to place. From couch to bed, from bed to floor. She never went far, her aching body protesting with every movement. The television had been on, set to the same channel, for days. Miranda had stared at it for hours without any comprehension of what flashed across the screen.

Her mind was obsessed now with that one word: *always.*

Somewhere in that tiny part of her brain which remembered her real life, she knew that William would be home soon. She knew that when that happened, one of two things would transpire.

Either the wondrous haunting would continue, and she would have much explaining to do, explaining that would probably cause her husband to leave her, if he didn't just lock her away in a psych ward somewhere first. The other option was even more terrible to think about: the haunting would stop. Daniel would be gone. Forever.

But there was another option. A way for them to be together. A way for her to have Daniel with her, pressed against her, inside her.

Always.

The news droned on in the background, voices drifting from the living room and dispersing throughout the halls of the house like well-informed echoes. The meteorologist took his three-minute slot to inform people that the cold front would not be abating any time soon, that temperatures were due to plummet into the negatives overnight, and that everyone should stay indoors unless going out was absolutely necessary and remember to leave their faucets dripping.

Miranda stretched out, motionless, at the bottom of the stairs. It had taken all her strength to crawl there on her hands and knees. Her body was heavy; her skin bore the telltale bruises of days of wild and violent lovemaking, and her mind floated somewhere dark and numb.

After a time, Miranda gathered the strength to sit up. She leaned heavily against the wall, pulled her knees to her chest, winced at the swollen pain between her legs. Through the picture window in the upstairs hall, she could see great fat flakes of snow swirling against a sunset sky. She watched these for a while, mesmerized, her mind drifting again.

As the great orange ball of the sun began to dip below the horizon and gale winds shook the windows, whistling around the corners of the house like long-lost lovers crying out for one another, Miranda slowly and quietly accepted her fate.

She rested a bit more. The work ahead would take every bit of her strength.

Finally, she rose. Her legs shook beneath her weight, but she propelled herself onward, one hand on the wall always lest she stumble.

She went methodically from room to room, performing the practiced motions of so many nights before, now in reverse. She opened every window as wide as it could go. The patio door slid until it hit the opposite wall, snow blowing in through the open space and immediately beginning to form small slushy mounds on the kitchen floor. Miranda shivered, cursing the way her body betrayed her.

She stood for a moment at the bottom of the stairs, looking up. Sixteen steps had never felt so daunting. Stumbling, crawling, one step at a time, she made her way slowly to the top. Again, she performed her rounds: opening every window, leaving every door wide. Finally, she stood before the thermostat mounted on the wall beside her bedroom door.

She flipped the switch resolutely.

Off.

Moonlight streamed in through the large windows of her bedroom as she pulled off her clothing. Jeans, shirt, panties, bra, socks; all dropped into a messy pile onto the gleaming wood floor. Miranda lay down on the bed, on her back, arms and legs spread in imitation of da Vinci's Vitruvian Man, laid out now as a sacrifice to insatiable desire.

Miranda willed herself to lay perfectly still, to relax. The blankets at her back held a warmth which both comforted and annoyed her. The reserved heat would only make it take longer, but she no longer had the strength to do anything about it.

The wind blew, cold and cruel, into the house. Snow mounded beneath each window and formed great drifts beside the patio door. The temperature began to drop, slowly at first, the heater's last few breaths struggling against nature's unconquerable strength.

Within hours, the pale green glow of the thermostat read thirty-eight degrees, the number changing, dropping, every few minutes.

Stretched out on her bed, Miranda's body twitched and jerked violently, desperate to generate its own warmth in whatever way possible. She squeezed her eyes closed and gritted her teeth against the urge to curl up, to wrap her arms around her body and preserve those vital organs held within.

By midnight, the thermostat read sixteen degrees. Miranda's body no longer shivered. Her skin had taken on a pale and waxy sheen, the many bruised handprints standing out in stark relief. Her muscles were stiff, almost rigid; her hands and feet had moved from a tingling numbness to a point where she could not feel them at all. They might have disappeared altogether as far as she knew.

In her distant and drifting thoughts, Miranda pictured her extremities slowly vaporizing, hanging frozen in the air above the bed in a vaguely body-shaped collection of ice crystals, and the thought made her laugh.

Miranda drifted. The night was an ocean of cold darkness that wrapped itself lovingly around her. She was weightless, rocking back and forth on waves of oblivion. She no longer knew if her eyes were open or closed; all was a void of peaceful twilight either way.

The sun rose. Pale pink light fell across the bed, across Miranda's body, her ivory skin now tinted a disturbing shade of blue.

She felt the light creep across her, felt it dig around beneath her eyelids, trying to find a way in. She wanted to turn her head away from it, wanted to block out the glow and the slight warmth it might carry, but she no longer had any control over her body.

Nothing moved, no matter how much she willed it to. If she stretched her consciousness, she could just hear the slow and broken beat of her heart. It sounded like a wounded thing, a damaged thing, a thing just on the edge of admitting defeat.

But still, it beat on.

Hours passed. The sun rose high in the sky, and the temperature inside the house warmed a few degrees. Miranda did not have the presence of mind to be upset by this delay.

Just past noon, the prayers she would have whispered had her lips not been frozen found an answer: great banks of slate-gray clouds moved in, obscuring the sun, blocking both its light and its heat. The wind picked up again; the temperature dropped quickly.

Into this swirl of wind and cold and snow came the presence Miranda had been waiting for.

She felt Daniel's caress against her numb skin. For once, his touch was not freezing; it seemed to warm her instead. A sigh which crystallized above her lips escaped from deep inside her.

Miranda forced herself to open her eyes, squinting against the small amount of light which still suffused the room. In the gloom a shadow loomed over her. She recognized its contours immediately: the long legs, the broad shoulders, the head tilted slightly to the side.

Daniel. The word flew inside her mind, unable to find its way to her lips.

The bed shifted beneath her as the shadow climbed atop her.

Warmth spread throughout her body, a smoldering ember in that sacred space between her legs, radiating heat outward. Her heart tapped out a drumroll of panicked beats inside her chest.

Deep within, she felt the pulse of Daniel's thrusts. Miranda's eyes rolled back as the pressure of his hands pushed against her throat.

This was it. This was what she had been waiting for, hoping for. This was the fulfillment of the desire she would die for.

Miranda's body lay, perfectly still, in the freezing house. The wind which careened around the outside corners blew into the room, lifting the curtains in a ghostly dance.

Snow sat upon the windowsill, upon the dresser. A glaze of ice frosted over the mirror which sat in the corner of the room, distorting the reflection of the dying woman upon the bed.

Ice crystals fringed her eyelashes; her lips were fading from the dark blue of a winter midnight to the paler shade of a summer sunrise.

Her body did not move. No shadow overtook her. But in Miranda's mind, in those last few moments of firing synapses before her heart stuttered out its last weak pulse, Daniel surrounded her.

His arms made a cage on either side of her head; the heavy length of his body pinned her to the mattress. His hips thrust against her, slow but hard, and she moaned with each imagined movement.

In her mind she heard his voice, felt the wet heat of his breath against her ear.

Come for me, honey. Come for me.

I own you, Miranda. You are mine.

Tell me you're mine. Say my name.

Her lips cracked; cold, sluggish blood oozed from the fissures as her mouth formed the words.

"I'm yours, Daniel. I'm yours."

Miranda's heart gave one final, feeble thump. The scene in her mind faded, blackened at the edges, snuffed out like a candle flame.

The last fragile heat in her body released, dissipating into the frigid air.

I'm.

Yours.

Daniel.

They were not words, merely thoughts, feelings, feathers of awareness that caught in the air of Miranda's dying breath and floated, weightless, into the dark distance beyond.

DUST

I am dust.
See me there upon the highest
  Hard to reach shelf,
In the back corners of curio cabinets,
Caught on the stilled blade of a ceiling fan,
Mixed with yellow pollen along the windowsill.

I am dust.
The soft gray accompaniment
  To a life lived.
Parts of me – skin cells and hair,
Bits of my clothing, dirt from bare feet,
Left behind in the places I have been.

I am dust.
Caught in the cracks of the window
  In my childhood bedroom
Where I sat for long hours
With a book in my hand, in the maple tree's shade.
Maple leaf, book page, and me: we are dust.

Echoes of the Dead

I am dust.
Lying quiet on the back high shelf
  Of my teenage-years closet
Where I hid pages of poetry
And scandalous photographs behind school awards.
The pages, the photos, and me: we are dust.

I am dust.
Stirred by spring winds and autumn rains
  In the forest I roamed years ago,
Where I walked as I pondered the mysteries of life
And I cried over loves lost and longings denied.
The trees, the rocks, and me: we are dust.

I am dust.
In the sharp corners of crosses
  Carved into old pews
That I passed as I walked down a carpeted aisle
In a dress made of white lace and dreams.
The dress, the dreams, and me: we are dust.

I am dust.
Stubbornly lingering in a bright, sterile room
  In a hospital somewhere uptown
Where I breathed and I groaned and I pushed
And I moaned as I brought forth new life.
The nurses, the blankets, and me: we are dust.

I am dust.
In every playground and zoo and museum and park
  Within a day's drive of my house
Where I brought my children to play and to learn,
Where most of the days of my life disappeared.
The swing sets, the paintings, and me: we are dust.

Heather Daughrity

I am dust.
Sifted through the cracks of wooden back deck
  To lie silent on dark ground below,
There where he stood waiting for me to return,
Where he asked what was wrong and I said we were through.
The decking, the ex-love, and me: we are dust.

I am dust.
Caught in the folds of dark blue sheets
  On the bed where I now sleep alone,
Where I've burrowed and cried till I felt I would die,
Where I've dared to dream of love once again.
The pillows, the teardrops, and me: we are dust.

I am dust.
A devilish dervish in the corners
  Of the room where he first touched me,
Where I knew once again how it feels to be wanted,
Where we lay in the darkness and proclaimed our love.
The blankets, my lover, and me: we are dust.

I am dust.
Settled between the keyboard's keys
  And atop the stacked notebooks,
On the desk where I sit to spill my thoughts,
In the corner where my imagination stirs to life.
The pens, the pages, and me: we are dust.

I am dust.
Small pieces of myself left behind
  In all the places my life has paused.
Even now the dust of me mixes with others,
New little girls, lovelorn women, tired mothers.
Little by little we leave ourselves behind: ashes and dust.

DISSONANCE

There was nothing wrong with the bathroom; nothing that could be seen, anyway. The tiles were straight and white. The faucets, the showerhead, the knobs for hot and cold – all gleamed silver.

No soap scum stained the shower walls, no fingerprints or grime marred a single inch of surface. Cheerful sunlight filtered in through the lace curtains. The mirror over the sink reflected a perfect, unsmudged picture of peaceful bliss.

Still, I did not like to use the room. I did not like to enter it at all. Had my thoughts been logical, I would have kept the door at the end of the hall closed, banishing the bathroom to *out of sight, out of mind.* But my thoughts were not logical; they were scattered, unfocused, anxious.

The idea of closing that door, of leaving the bathroom to its own devices, bothered me more than the feel of the room's gaze falling on me every time I passed through the hall.

And I *did* feel that gaze. The room seemed alive, a dark consciousness hiding within it, cloaked just beneath all that gleaming white tile.

So, the door stayed open, the room within a shining, sterile reminder of all my failures folded into one unthinkably horrible and tragic moment.

I don't know how long it had taken me to get the room clean. I couldn't keep track of time in those days. Minutes dragged like hours and days sped by like seconds. It was winter; the constantly clouded sky, the late sunrises and early sunsets, the utter lack of any real distinction between day and night wrapped the house in a cocoon of soft, dusky light that felt both safe and suffocating.

It had been such a mess in the beginning. All those tiny hexagon tiles – *oh, how important that period-appropriate detail had been to me, back when I cared about such things*.

The crimson-brown blood had soaked into the grout, making paths across the bathroom floor like a map to a treasure no one should ever find.

Damn those tiny tiles, and damn the miles of grout between them.

The bathroom stares at me even now. I stand at the opposite end of the hall, six feet of daunting space between me and my bedroom door. The dim hall light flickers, and in the spastic shadows a darkness reaches from the black rectangle that is the bathroom doorway. I don't move, can't move, can't force myself away from this spot on the hardwood, my clammy feet sticking to the maple floorboards as long arms of shadow stretch along the walls, inching closer and closer.

I blink, and the spectral arms are gone. My chest rises and falls slowly, steadily, a studied act of normalcy.

Just breathe. I've told myself this a thousand times.

Just breathe, just breathe, just breathe. I've repeated the mantra enough, it seems, over the last six months, that my body now obeys this basic command with a calmness that belies the panic I swallow down, choking on my own fear.

My own guilt.

I remember when she first told me. I was sitting on the front porch, the fans overhead spinning lazily in the humid air, barely disturbing the heat of the late summer afternoon.

She came out and sat next to me. Her body was poised tensely, barely sitting at all, an animal approaching a possible trap, ready to spring away at any moment should the danger become real.

I set aside my gardening catalogs, arranging my face in an expression that I hoped didn't show my irritation at being interrupted. She was my only child, the product of a naïve teenage fling, fathered by a man who had spent more of the last twenty years in prison than out.

I had been the good girl – church girl, honor roll girl, my mail at sixteen filled with both college recruitment brochures and invitations to beauty pageants. He had been the antithesis of all that – the boy from the wrong side of the tracks, dark and dangerous, and to my teenage mind, in need of just a little love to make him into the man he should be.

My God, the scandal when I ended up pregnant. The whispers. The stares. The full brunt of scrutiny falling on me, while his buddies merely congratulated him. No one expected any different from him. Me, though… I had turned some people's whole damn world upside down.

We stayed together until just after her first birthday. He called me from a friend's house – and I say "friend" with all the scrutiny you can fit into one word – to tell me he had taken multiple bottles of pills and just wanted to say good-bye. I proceeded to yell at him over the phone. *Don't you dare do this to me, don't you dare leave me!*

My parents drove out and dragged him from that run-down trailer he'd decided to die in. They took him to the hospital where he was forced to choke down some activated charcoal and was admitted to the thirteenth floor – rehab.

I visited him every day. The withdrawal – because he'd been on more drugs than I'd even heard of – was hard.

Even harder was the moment, three days into his rehabilitation period, when I showed up to visit only to be told that he had checked himself out. I called his house. His brother answered, told me that my boyfriend, the father of my child, had decided I was better off without him.

When he called me a few days later to apologize and beg me to take him back, I repeated his own words to him: I – no, *we,* MY child and I – were better off without him.

I was not going to raise my daughter in that kind of situation.

She was raised apart from him, except for a few times, each years apart, when he decided he was going to clean up and be a father. Those episodes lasted a month or two at best. No, he'd never been any consistent part of her life.

But she was still so damn much like him.

She sat next to me on that porch, and what she said slammed an icepick of disbelief and dread into my heart.

She told me who she wanted to be.

No.

Sorry.

They told me who they wanted to be.

I hear the sounds at night, sometimes.

Lying alone in my bed, I'll come rushing up out of a drug-dead sleep, clutching at the blankets, eyes wide and heart pounding.

I wasn't there when it happened, of course. I wasn't in the room with her –

– *them.*

I was right here, sleeping safe and secure and self-righteous in my bed, while my dau–

    – my *child*

    – was down the hall, in that bathroom, doing the unthinkable.

I don't know what it sounds like when razors slice into thin, tender skin. Not really. But I know the sounds that echo down the hall in the darkness. The *skkkkrrrrtt* as the blade punctures and pulls.

One line. One line of beading red along a pale forearm.

Two lines.

Three.

A pause.

Slower now: three more lines on the opposite arm.

Is that a gasp? A quick, sharp inhale of breath at the pain of splitting flesh?

Beyond the gasps, sobs.

Quiet, controlled, heartbreaking sobs.

My child, my baby, falling apart, coming undone, so deep into the helpless depths of their own mind with no one to help pull them out.

No one. No one to help.

No one.

Their mother, asleep down the hall.

And them, so utterly, horribly alone.

They threw themselves fully into this new identity. Not new to them, apparently, but completely new to me.

Flags appeared on their bedroom walls. Rainbow stripes. One with baby blue, shell pink, and white.

I visited them at work one day, and the letters on their name tag were all mixed up, the name I'd given them gone, lost forever to some place that only I remembered with fondness; a new word, a new name had taken its place.

Their closet changed, too. The dresses they'd always hated – that I'd always insisted on – were gone. Every piece of clothing that I'd bought for them over the last few years magically disappeared, replaced with ripped black jeans, T-shirts with snarky sayings and band logos, and combat boots.

I cried. I cried and I cried and I cried.

I spent hours sitting in the darkness, my mind a tangled mess of thoughts. What had I done wrong? How had my child turned out this way? Had I been too strict or not strict enough? I had preached tolerance, glad to support people's happiness from a distance, but now that a great writhing mass of life-changing dissonance had landed right in my own lap, that tolerance was suddenly much harder to come by.

I worried for my child's soul. Forty years of church talk flooded my brain, words of judgment and condemnation, images of fire and brimstone. In turning their own life toward something new, was my child turning their back on the God they'd been raised to believe in? Did they still believe in God at all? If I gave in to their requests, if I accepted their new identity, was I condemning my child to eternal damnation?

I could not process the conflicting thoughts and ideas that battled in my brain.

I went numb.

Absolutely numb.

I see the blood. It starts in my periphery. A drop here, a splattered cluster there. A spot of crimson red on the pure white of the bathroom floor, or the side of the tub. That one heartbreaking smear along the wall.

Not always in the bathroom, though, no.

Drops on my snow-white bedspread.

Flecks of red on the petals of the gardenias outside the front door.

Smears of scarlet on every wall of every room I ever venture inside.

Water is becoming hard to deal with as well.

The first time the water bloomed with blood, I was washing dishes down in the kitchen. It was just me eating these days, and barely that; using the dishwasher for one plate, one cup, one fork seemed ridiculous. So, I'd taken to rinsing and stacking the dishes for a day or three and then washing them by hand, up to my elbows in soapy water, my eyes fixed somewhere in the distance beyond the window above the sink.

I glanced down, my hands swirling through the murky water, checking for any remaining forks or knives.

I paused, blinked hard to make sure I wasn't imagining things or seeing some strange trick of the light.

I worried for a moment that I had unknowingly cut myself on the tip of a knife. I hadn't broken any dishes, had I? There wasn't a shattered plate, a collection of sharp and jagged edges hidden in that water, just waiting to slice me open, was there?

I raised my hands from the water.

They dripped red.

Bubbles in shades of pain and guilt and *oh, God, my baby, my poor baby*.

The kitchen sink. The tub. The pool.

The goddamn tank of lobsters at the supermarket.

All streaked with blood.

Oh, the conversations we had. Over text. Over stupid, goddamn text, because neither of us were brave enough to confront the other face to face.

We lived in the same house, walked the same floors, went out the same door every morning and night, but we became like ghosts to one another. The few words we exchanged were trivial things. *Good morning. Good night. We're almost out of milk.*

But when she – sorry, damn it – *they* were gone, off to work or out with all their new friends, it was then, *then, when we were far from each other,* that we'd muster up the courage to haul out the big issues.

I couldn't get past myself. I was stuck in a straitjacket of thoughts and opinions and so damn terrified of what these changes meant for *me* that I could not see what it meant for *them*.

I could not be the mother my child needed.

They were so alone.

I couldn't see it then, but I see it now.

So utterly alone.

The dreams are getting worse now. Nightmares in monochrome. Blindingly white tiles. The stygian darkness crowding every corner. And the ever-present red, that startlingly, painfully bright crimson of their blood.

I rise from my bed at the sound of water. Not the soft and gentle sloshing of someone in a tub, no, this is the sound of great ocean waves crashing on a rocky shore. I tiptoe from my bedroom. The hallway beyond stretches impossibly long, the path from my door to the bathroom lengthening exponentially faster than my feet can carry me. My tentative steps turn to panicked running.

From the room at the end of the hall a new sound emerges, a soft, breathy gasp of pain that echoes endlessly along the walls of this godforsaken corridor. I run faster.

The gasps are joined by sobs, those quiet, quiet sobs, like she – they – *damn it*, HE – knew that they –

– *HE*

– was all alone, that no one would come, that a cry for help was useless, pointless, that their –

– *HIS*

– mother had abandoned

– *HIM*.

I found him the next morning. The water gone cold, the light of a winter sunrise bathing the whole room in a pale pink glow. He hadn't undressed; he hated his own body right till the end. He lay slumped sideways in the tub, his head resting against the side. There was only a foot of water, dark red, soaked into his clothes. His left arm hung over the side of the tub nearest me, the puddle of cooling blood beneath it somehow less tragic than that one accusing smear on the opposite wall, a testament to the last movement my child –

– *my son*

– ever made.

Had he rethought his decision in the end? Had he tried to stand up, to call for me, haul himself out of the tub and crawl down the hallway seeking help from the one person in his life he should have been able to count on to love and accept him, no matter what?

Had he died there, in that tub of lukewarm water and his own lifeblood, thinking that he had failed me, that he had been abandoned, discarded, forsaken? Did he really, truly, feel that he was alone?

Was he?

Was he alone? Had I abandoned him?

Oh, God, how could I live with myself?

I've decided to stop avoiding the bathroom.

I sit in the tub, alone.

Dry.

Warm in the June sunshine pouring in through the window.

Not cold, not wet, not alone in the dark of a winter night like he was.

Not lying back against chilled porcelain, so utterly hopeless that I see no point in living.

But close.

Oh, so close.

I sit cross-legged in the tub, my back to the wall where I know the smear will never fully disappear. I lean forward, my arms folded over the side of the tub, looking down. My eyes scan the tracks between the floor's hexagon tiles, searching for the tiny particles of blood that I know must still live there. Tears fall unhindered, saltwater coursing through those same tracks.

I don't have a razor blade. I'm not that brave. But I do have a collection of orange pill bottles. They'll give just about anything to a grieving mother to shut her up.

I'm sure if I can manage to swallow them down, I can curl up here in this tub, fall asleep, and never wake up.

Who am I to live when I forced my child to feel that their best option was to die?

I hold one of the pill bottles in my hand, turn it back and forth, back and forth between my fingers. I spend what feels like hours staring up at the window, my mind blissfully blank.

I'm emptying everything out. All thought, all judgment, all sorrow, all guilt. Every obligation or responsibility I've ever had, cut free. Every emotion processed, forgiven, set loose. There's nothing here for me. Not now. Not anymore.

I drop the pill bottle and pick up my phone. I pull up the last picture my son posted on social media. He looks completely different from his own self just a year earlier, with bright blue hair and a spiky piercing through his eyebrow, but I smile as I see those same deep, thoughtful eyes. The same little turn-up at the corner of the lips. The same scar on one cheek.

My child.

My baby.

My son.

I pour all the pills into the biggest bottle, cap it, shake it up. A lovely cocktail of forgetfulness and hopefully, forgiveness.

I open the bottle of water that's been sitting next to the tub, waiting, since I first came in here hours ago.

I pour the first half dozen pills into one hand, hold my phone – my son's picture – in the other.

I raise the pills to my mouth, forcing all thoughts, all distractions, from my mind.

The phone *pings*. A notification pops up, a gray box with black text across his picture.

A reminder.

An event I know, with complete certainty, that I did not put on my calendar.

It's June, and the local Pride Parade is tomorrow.

I lower the hand with the pills, pour them back into the bottle, cap it, and set it gently on the floor.

I look at his picture. The corner of his mouth seems turned up a little more, a knowing smirk playing at his lips. It seems... understanding, somehow.

Hopeful.

I stand on the sidewalk, feeling self-conscious, out of place, an imposter, but I'm determined to be brave. I've copied a sign I once saw in a picture; the posterboard I hold up says, simply: FREE MOM HUGS.

There's a wild, raucous, happy sort of feel to the whole event. Bright colors everywhere. I get a few smiles at first, a thumbs-up or two.

I stand there for half an hour before she first approaches me. It's clear she's somewhere mid-transition, a young woman barely more than a child. She seems to be there alone, shrinking into herself amid the noise and gleeful chaos. She walks up slowly, her eyes scanning the words of my sign over and over as if searching for some small print, some caveat.

I prop the sign on the bench behind me, and her eyes lift to mine. There's so much pain there, so much loneliness, that I feel a stone drop into my stomach. She's so close, walking so narrow a ledge.

I nod my head to her, lift my arms in welcome. She steps forward, wraps her own arms around me, tentatively at first. Then her body sags against mine, and her grip grows stronger, holding on to me for dear life.

"I'm so sorry," she says, trying to sniffle back the snot and tears that are soaking my shirt.

I cradle her head in my hand, keep holding her.

"It's okay," I say, my voice quiet, reassuring – I hope.

Her whole body shakes with a sob. "It's just… it's just… do you have any idea how awful it is to feel like no one understands you, no one gets you, no one accepts you, no one loves you?"

She's trembling now, a scared child lost at sea, holding on to anything that might keep her from drowning.

Drowning. A blood-red ocean contained in white porcelain.

I push the image from my mind, concentrate instead on the mischievous half-grin that I loved for every moment of my son's twenty years on this planet.

"I do," I tell her. "Not personally, but… but I love someone who once felt the same way, so I understand. As well as I can, anyway."

She stands there for a minute or two more, relaxed into my embrace, *just breathe-ing* herself into a state of semi-calm. I wait for her to pull away, happy to stand there all day if that's what it takes.

When she does step back, she offers me the smallest of smiles. "Thanks," she says, "I really needed that."

I give her my business card, tell her to call my number whenever she needs someone to talk to. I tell her she's welcome to come for dinner any time.

She wipes her nose on her sleeve, catches herself, and looks at me sheepishly, a kid caught doing something they know they're not supposed to do. I just smile.

She thanks me again, tucks the card into her pocket, nods her head, and disappears into the crowd.

I take a few deep breaths, wipe away the tears at the corners of my own eyes.

I scan the mass of people lining both sides of the street. There, on the opposite side, for a moment I swear I see a tall young man, bright blue hair and a quirky half-grin. His eyes meet mine, deep, thoughtful, approving… forgiving.

I blink and he's gone.

I turn, pick my sign up, and wait for the next hurting soul.

DEFENSES

Mel sat at the edge of the cliff.

A brisk spring wind pushed at her body and whipped her hair around her face. Below, a sharp drop of a hundred feet or more, and then, spread out between the cliff bottom and the distant town, the sloping mounds of Harper Hill Cemetery.

She liked to come here, always had, even as a child, though Lord knew she'd gotten in trouble for it enough times.

It was a good place for sitting and thinking. As a little girl she'd sometimes lay back on the grass and let her brain go fuzzy-sleepy, squinting up at the sunlight and daydreaming as she watched clouds scud by overhead. Sometimes she'd bring an old quilt, a book, and a snack, and spend an hour or two reading.

Mostly, though, she'd sit, just like she was now, legs drawn up to her chest, arms wrapped around her knees, and gaze down at the graveyard below, letting her mind wander.

Her thoughts were far different today than the ones she'd had as a child, of course. Adulthood had a way of doing that at the best of times, without benefit of the story she'd just heard, a story that, if she chose to believe it were true, was the most weirdly intriguing thing she'd ever heard.

Grandma Birdie wasn't necessarily one to be trusted these days, not now that her mind had begun to wander down the long-neglected hallways of distant memory.

There were days when she didn't recognize Mel, her own granddaughter, when she came to visit. There had even been days when she had taken one look at Mel and begun shrieking, pointing a shaking finger accusingly at the young woman and accusing her, with trembling voice, of stealing her face.

Birdie's nurse would come rushing in then, doing her best to soothe the old woman, tempting her away from the offending situation with promises of hot tea and cookies. Mel knew that the tea would be used to wash down one of the pills her grandmother sometimes took, the ones that calmed her down and made her sleep for hours afterward. Birdie would wake up later that day and smile at her granddaughter like nothing had happened.

The signs were slight, at first. Little slips in her thinking, little dips back into events that happened days or years before. Then she began to forget things, important things, and to mix up the real and the imagined, the past and the present.

Still, there were times when the old woman seemed more or less lucid, and today had been one of those days. Today, when she had told the story, Birdie had seemed more clear and confident in her words than Mel had seen her in a long time.

Could it be true, though? Could it actually have happened?

Mel let her grandmother's words run through her mind once again…

I was so young then; young and beautiful and carefree. We were in love, your grandfather and I, madly yet innocently in love with each other. I had known he was the one for me from the moment I laid eyes on him at the age of fifteen. Oh, he was tall and golden and charming. And so mischievous! He was always playing the most exasperatingly clever tricks on me.

We knew we would get married some day; we just had to wait until we were old enough. My parents threw a big party, my official "coming out" into society as an eligible young woman. I don't care what anyone else says, the real point of those silly parties was to show off a young lady to all the available bachelors in the area. It never occurred to me, however, that anyone other than my beautiful Paul would be interested in my hand.

But someone was.

James Lucas was ten years my senior. He owned a modest house and a more-than-modest spread of arable land just a couple of miles down the road. He had grown up well-off, then struck out, determined to make his own name without the help of his father, and he had been surprisingly successful already.

James was tall, taller than your grandfather, but lanky; thin bones held together with long muscles and ropy tendons. He was handsome in his own right, don't you get me wrong. He had dark hair and even darker eyes. And he was *also* charming, in a mysterious and brooding kind of way.

I must admit, even though I knew I loved your grandfather, Paul, there was a little thrill of excitement and danger in the knowledge that James Lucas also desired me as his wife.

I'm not proud of it, but I entertained his attentions for a while. I pretended that I did it out of obligation; *of course* my father would want me to at least consider James's advances.

I flirted with him, but what I didn't know was that I was really flirting with danger.

For three months, I was courted – officially – by both Paul and James. I never once truly considered James as an option for marriage, but my silly girlish mind liked the time, the attention, and the wooing that he offered me. I would spend three evenings of each week with your grandfather and one with James. I would joke to my friends that I was simply "keeping things interesting."

I knew Paul didn't like the situation, but I also knew that he had been brought up properly and would never act in any way unbecoming a gentleman. I watched him swallow his jealousy so many times. And I will admit: it gave me a little thrill, every time we would come into James's proximity, while walking in town or at some dance or gathering or another. Paul's eyes would narrow, his jaw clench, and his arm would tighten protectively, possessively, around my waist.

I had no idea what I was doing. I did not comprehend then the power that a woman can have over men's hearts and actions.

I was simply playing around with another person's emotions, and I'm so horribly ashamed of it, now.

I knew that Paul's proposal would come at any moment; I had a feeling that he would drop to one knee at Christmas, knowing how much I loved the holiday, and ask for my hand in marriage, which of course I had every intention of giving.

What I did not expect was that James would beat him to it.

At the Andersons' annual harvest celebration, surrounded by pumpkins and apples and dried corn shocks, I took turns dancing with both Paul and James. I was hot, flushed and flustered, gasping for breath and desperate for a drink, when James swept me out of the house and into the dying gardens beyond.

He pulled me close against him, almost violently, and my breath hitched in my throat at the forcefulness and the closeness. He kissed me then, the first kiss we'd shared, and it was so beautifully sad and desperate that for the briefest moment I kissed him back. Then he backed away quickly and pulled a small box from his pocket.

There, under the autumn moon, with bonfires spotting the hills in the distance, he asked me to marry him.

It was in that moment that I began to realize the danger of what I had done. What had been merely a game for me had been something very serious for him. But I couldn't marry him. I was going to marry your grandfather; there had never been the slightest doubt in my mind about it.

I told him "no" as gently as I could. He stood before me in silence for a moment, his jaw working back and forth and his gaze intense. Confusion, and then pain, passed across his features, and then something else, something darker: anger.

He grabbed my arms, hard and rough, and held me in place. His fingers dug into the soft flesh just above my elbows, and I cried out in pain. James opened his mouth to speak, his breath hot and hateful against my face, but whatever words he had for me were never spoken.

Paul appeared in that moment, as if he had materialized from the darkness itself, an imposing specter, the triumphant anger in his own eyes rivalling the pained rage in James's. Paul pushed James away from me, pushed him again and again, telling him to keep his hands off me, to never dare to touch me again, in fact, to never dare come into my presence again.

James backed up, but he did not back down. As I stood shivering from cold and fear, the two men passed further and further away from me, until they were just two shapeless forms in the distant dark.

I heard Paul speak, the words too quiet to make out but his voice full of confidence and threat. James responded, his own tones low and menacing; a few words, and then he turned on his heel and strode away, beyond the reach of the light from the guttering gas lamps which surrounded the Andersons' home, into the night.

Your grandfather came back to me then, pressing me against him in an embrace which was every bit as crushing as the way James had held me, but in Paul's arms I felt only safe and loved.

Whatever schemes he had concocted for an elaborate proposal went out the window. The very next day, Paul appeared at our house asking to speak with my father. They spent half an hour sequestered in Daddy's study before reappearing from that smoky no-woman's-land, smiling and shaking hands and thumping each other on the back. A small velvet box appeared in Paul's fingers and he dropped to one knee in front of me, right there in the front parlor, and asked for my hand in marriage while my mother and sister looked on, swooning, in the background.

Of course I said yes.

The wedding was set for the first day of spring, and the women of the house flew into motion in preparation of a grand affair.

We did not see James again, save for a few times when his dark, brooding form passed across the opposite end of the street in town. He never came near, though, never attempted to speak to me, whether Paul was with me or not. When Paul *was* with me, though, his eyes would narrow, his gaze locked on his competitor, his hands curling into clenched fists until James would pass from sight.

April thirteenth, one week before the wedding, a huge storm began to build off in the west. The wind blew all day, growing in intensity as the afternoon stretched toward evening and great black clouds rolled up to dizzying heights in the skies overhead. Bright streaks of lightning bounced from cloud to cloud in the distance, and growling rumbles of thunder shook the ground as Paul and I hurried toward the shelter of his house – *this* house.

We rushed inside just in time, fat drops of rain beginning to strike the roof of the porch moments after we ducked beneath its sheltering cover. The glow of the setting sun disappeared completely, dropping below the horizon in a fanfare of fiery light as the sky went dark. It seemed almost as if the clouds had descended to circle your grandfather's estate, cutting us off from the outside world completely.

There was a tenseness in Paul's stance, an awareness of danger that did not seem to be due entirely to the oncoming storm. He pushed me through the door before him, then turned, his body a shield between me and the outside world, and looked intently all around, as if he thought some danger lurked in the rain-pelted dark.

Here, Grandma Birdie had paused, gazing blankly off into the distance, her mind clearly somewhere, or some*time,* else. Mel had been enthralled by the tale, even as she questioned its truth. Birdie was fading out now, that far-off glassiness beginning to descend over her eyes, but Mel still had questions.

"Well, I know you and Grandpa Paul got married. Obviously. But Grandma, what about the other guy? What about James?"

Birdie's eyes – and mind – had slid slowly back into the present, her gaze finally finding focus on Mel's face.

He disappeared that very night, never to be seen or heard from again.

Mel scoffed at this obvious falsehood, this easy way out. Birdie's eyes began to drift again, and Mel followed the line of her grandmother's sight to the cliff beyond the window, and the steep drop to the graveyard below.

That's what everyone else thought, at least. But your grandfather and I knew better.

We had only been inside for a few minutes, Paul stoking up the fire to warm the chill from our bones, when a slow, echoing knock sounded on the front door. Paul's face settled into hard lines at the sound, as if a doom he had been anticipating for a long time had finally come calling, and now he must face it.

Birdie had grown agitated then, her gaze drifting sideways again, hands lifting and dropping aimlessly.

"I didn't... We couldn't... We never...."

The old woman's voice had grown louder, rising in pitch until she sounded like a frightened child. The nurse had come in then, making her shushing noises and touching Birdie lightly but firmly, guiding her toward the back of the house with practiced gentleness.

Tea and cookies and sedatives had calmed her grandmother, and now Mel was taking a few calming breaths of her own at her spot near the edge of the cliff while Birdie slept. She was intrigued by the story, impatient to hear the ending but hesitant to bring it up again. There was a good chance that Birdie would wake up with no recollection of telling the tale. There was an equally good chance that it had been just that: a tale and nothing more.

But Mel felt a strange sense of truth and reality to the story, and she made up her mind to try to gently, carefully coax the ending from her grandmother's rattled old brain before the night was over.

A strange, moaning wind caressed the corners of the house as the three women – Mel, Birdie, and the nurse, Maggie – sat down to dinner together. Birdie, despite her nap, still seemed restless, anxious, confused. By the time Maggie cleared the dishes away, straightened the kitchen, and came into the sitting room to say goodnight, dark clouds had obscured the silver crescent of the moon. Mel watched as the first drops of rain speckled the fabric of Maggie's top as she hurried to her car.

Mel tucked an afghan around Birdie's frail legs. The rain fell in waves beyond the windows, rising and falling in volume, as Mel settled into the chair across from her grandmother. She licked her lips, took a deep breath, and begged for the rest of the story.

Birdie sunk into the chair, her shoulders rounding and rising, arms crossed in front of her, knees pressed tight together beneath the blanket. She spent a moment staring out the window. Mel watched as the present fell away from her grandmother's eyes, as they focused on another time, long ago…

I knew, somehow, knew by the look on Paul's face, by the icy prickling in my own veins, who was on the other side of that door. Paul opened the door slowly, the steady roar of the rain rushing into the hall and echoing off the high walls. Beyond the meager light that spilled from the door stood a figure, tall, dark, hooded and cloaked.

James.

Paul stepped forward, a determined grimace on his face. He pulled the door shut behind him, closing me inside alone while he and James faced each other in the flooded night.

Of course, I ran to the window immediately. The men stood in the deluge, both gesturing madly, their angry shouts whipped away by the howling wind. James pulled something from beneath his cloak. It took me a moment to realize what it was, but as I squinted into the darkness beyond the rain-lashed window, I recognized the shape of a gun.

I screamed then, loud enough that the men heard me over the sound of the storm. James's head jerked toward the window I stood behind. Paul took his moment; while James was looking at me, Paul grabbed the gun with both hands. James resisted; for a moment it seemed as if Paul would not be able to wrestle the gun from him.

In the end, Paul proved the stronger, but as he wrenched backward with all his might to pull the weapon from James's grasp, he lost his balance, slipping and sprawling in the mud, the gun flying from his hand and landing somewhere beyond the pools of light cast by the porch lanterns.

It was a mad scramble then, both men fighting and tripping over one another, trying to find the gun, trading wild punches as they went. Further and further from the house they searched, running and stumbling and pushing each other down.

Finally, they reached the edge of the cliff. James must have given up hope of finding the gun; instead, he reached beneath his cloak again and this time the object he pulled out was unmistakable, its long blade flashing silver in the lightning which split the sky behind them.

They grappled together there on the edge of the cliff, wrestling for control of the knife. James's arm plummeted downward; Paul's knees buckled, his body falling face-first into the mud.

I screamed again. I was sure James meant to kill him. I could not let that happen. Against all sense, I wrenched the door open and ran out into the night myself, toward the cliff and the man I loved. I struggled, the mud pulling at my feet as I pushed on, determined to reach Paul, to placate James, to get help, to… I didn't know. I only knew I could not leave Paul alone there.

I threw myself over Paul's body. The knife handle still stuck out from his right shoulder; he had propped himself up on his left elbow, his right arm useless. James stood, a tall silhouette against the stormy sky. He leaned forward, toward Paul, and I did my best to shield him.

But James was no longer concerned with Paul; it was me he wanted. He grabbed me by the arm, yanking me up, pressing me tight against him, his body radiating frenzied heat through his soaking clothes. He spoke only one word: *Mine*. He snarled a sort of victorious growl into my ear, then turned away from Paul, pulling me with him.

Something overcame me then. I've tried for sixty years to put a name to that feeling, and I haven't yet found a word adequate to it. It was a mixture of rage and fear, panic and disgust and terror at what might await me if I allowed James to drag me off somewhere. A strength I had never known – and have not known since – swelled up inside me, a blind fury of self-preservation.

I was all flailing limbs – arms and legs striking and kicking out at anything I could reach. Your grandfather later said that I looked like a true whirling dervish that night. Somehow, in the chaos that my body had become, I broke away from the man who held me, but I was not content to simply be free. I turned on him, Mel. I turned on him and I ran at him with all the speed and outrage I had within me, and I pushed him.

He toppled backward at the unexpected force, and every time he tried to rise up, I knocked him back over, pushing and kicking at him, acting purely on some survival instinct I did not know I possessed. I backed him further and further toward Paul, toward the cliff, toward the drop-off.

Then it happened.

He made to stand, one last time, and with every bit of strength I had, like a woman possessed, I planted my feet ankle-deep in the mud, and I pushed him.

Over the edge.

He didn't scream, didn't make a sound as he plummeted to the ground. In my mind, his body must have made a horrible crunch as he landed atop one of the gravestones in the cemetery below, but if it did, the noise was lost beneath the tumult of the storm.

Here, Birdie paused, and the dreaminess in her eyes grew stronger. Her words began to trail off as she finished the tale, sentences fading into nothingness.

"I got him in... patched him up... Still in our wet clothes... Down the hill... the body, the horrible angles of the broken... Took us hours, hours to dig... Gone... Disappeared... Never seen again."

The old woman began to tremble, violent spasms which shook her whole body. Mel's concern for her grandmother's immediate safety overrode her shock at the story; she quickly put together a cup of warm tea – and a sedative. Once the medication had begun to take effect, she helped Birdie to bed, tucking in extra blankets around her grandmother's chin.

Beyond the window, rain continued to fall, its steady hiss punctuated now and then with rumbles of thunder and cracks of lightning. Birdie's eyelids were growing heavy, her frenzied breathing slowing to something less frightening, as she trained her eyes on the window.

"I think he's still out there sometimes, in the storm," she whispered, her voice so quiet that Mel had to lean in close to the old woman's mouth to make out the words.

"I swear I see him sometimes, out there, a tall, dark shadow against the night, a spirit climbed up from the base of the cliff, waiting for his chance to... to finish... what he..."

Birdie's eyes closed; the hands which had gripped so tightly at the blankets relaxed. Mel straightened up and sat for a few moments longer on the edge of her grandmother's bed, not willing to admit to herself that her eyes searched for something out in the night, in the dark, in the storm.

Mel returned to the sitting room, intending to tidy up a bit, but instead she sank back into the chair she had occupied earlier while listening to her grandmother's story.

She would give herself a few moments to settle, to process what she had just heard.

The ancient grandfather clock in the hall woke her as it struck midnight, its twelve sonorous booms echoing through the house with the ominous foreboding of a death knell. Goosebumps skittered their way down Mel's skin. She rose slowly, dizzy, and walked toward the window.

This must have been the same window Gran stood at as she watched the two men on the cliff.

Mel peered out into the darkness. Rain still fell steadily, and Mel knew that already the ground between the house and the cliff would be a great sucking mess of mud.

There.

What was that? That shape near the spot where the cliff dropped off to the cemetery below? It looked like…

A man. A tall, dark man in a cloak.

No.

Fear coursed through Mel's veins like poison, acid-green and toxic, neutralizing all logical thought.

A voice sounded in her head, quiet, seductive. It spoke to her without words, with sensations which flowed through her body, burning away the fear.

Mel opened the front door. She stepped outside. Her bare feet squelched in the mud as she made her way to the cliff, to the figure that waited for her there, beckoning, whispering strange promises in her mind.

James Lucas waited for her. She knew this with an irrational certainty, knew that this meeting was inevitable, knew that he had waited for her for all these long, lonely years, denied his prize until this moment.

Mel made her way through the sucking mud until she stood face-to-face with the sinister specter on the cliff, willingly entering the embrace of its outstretched arms. Her heart beat fast; the world swam in and out of focus around her as an icy numbness trickled down her spine and into her arms and legs. She remained upright only through a will other than her own.

The voice in her head spoke again, a dizzying echo of deep, dark tones overlaid with rushing whispers.

Mine. Mine. Mine.

Mel could feel herself falling away, her consciousness slipping over the precipice that her body now stood so perilously close to. The specter's embrace tightened; Mel's vision blurred around the edges. She dropped further into the welcoming darkness...

"No!"

The shout came to her ears as if underwater, a warbling wave of distant sound, a sonic boom reverberating through her consciousness, knocking it loose from the trap it had fallen into.

Mel gasped, her eyes flying open. She looked up in horror at the figure that stood above her, but the figure's eyes were focused on something else. Mel turned her head in the same direction, as another infuriated cry split the night like lightning.

Mel's knees went out from under her at the sight.

Birdie, her eighty-year-old grandmother, flew toward them, her eyes lit with a wild, cold fire. The old woman's hands were outstretched, her gnarled fingers like claws at the end of bony arms.

The specter which stood over Mel shifted slightly, a tremor running through it, distorting its dark edges.

Mine, the dark shape whispered.

"Mine!" Birdie's voice spoke clear and loud. "You couldn't have me, and you can't have her!"

The old woman rushed toward them, passing by Mel as she sat, unable to move, on the muddy ground. Birdie crashed into the ghost of the man who had once asked for her hand in marriage, her momentum carrying them both up and over the edge of the cliff, and then...

Down.

Mel screamed. She scrambled as close to the edge as she dared, peering over into the darkness below. She could not see anything, no body, no pale shape against the ground where her grandmother's form should be.

Her grandmother. Birdie. How could that have been her? How could the frail woman Mel knew, the woman who couldn't get out of bed by herself, have run down the hill to the cliff, shouting her head off, and hit that man with enough force to knock him backward?

Mel shook her head. But he wasn't a man. He was a... what? A ghost?

Then, how could her grandmother have pushed a ghost over the edge of the cliff?

Unless...

The thought hit Mel with a sickening certainty.

She managed to stand up, legs unsteady beneath her as she made her way up the hill and back into the house. She did not stop to worry over the muddy footprints she left on the smooth floors as she hurried toward her grandmother's bedroom.

Mel turned the knob carefully and pushed the door open as quietly as she could. The room was silent but for the sound of the steadily lessening rain beyond the windows.

Mel approached the bed slowly. The shape beneath the blankets did not move. She extended a trembling hand, searching for the switch on the bedside lamp.

The room lit up, a soft, cozy glow, a spot of warmth and safety against the storm outside.

Birdie lay unmoving in her bed, her head turned toward the window, fast-dulling eyes fixed on the view of the cliff beyond.

Mel sank to the floor, her grandmother's small, wrinkled hand held in her own, and wept.

Melody "Birdie" Harper was laid to rest beside her husband in the family cemetery at the base of the looming cliff. Her granddaughter visited her grave each week, swapping out old, wilted flowers for new, vibrant ones. She sat for hours, sometimes thinking, sometimes talking aloud to whatever part of her grandmother might still remain.

And sometimes, when the evening sunlight drifted across the cemetery at just the right slant, a single ray would puncture the gloom of the woods that ringed the graveyard and shine with a diminished yet unmistakable light on an old, worn, man-sized mound of dirt; a grave unmarked, unknown, unloved.

DEMONS

Michael Fenton knew he was pushing his luck. He knew that if he drove just a little more slowly or stopped one more time for a bathroom break, he would not make it in time.

His mind wrestled with the idea of it: just let off the gas a bit, drive a mile or two under the speed limit, and he could arrive in Blackburn half an hour too late. Surely half an hour was all it would take; a funeral for a man few would care to mourn shouldn't take longer than that.

Michael could picture Diane's face, could feel the disappointment that would roll off her in waves if she found out he had missed it. He could hear her voice in his mind, scolding him in that weary way she had of talking, like just living with him exhausted her: "He's your father, Michael. Your father. How would you feel knowing your own son didn't care enough to show up to your funeral on time?"

Michael let out a small puff of air, a laugh that turned into a sigh before it escaped. He doubted his own son would show up to his funeral at all, with the way things were going between them these days. Nathan would probably throw a party instead.

With Diane's voice echoing in his head, Michael pressed down a little harder on the gas pedal. He adjusted the too-tight tie around his itching neck, shifted a bit in his seat, and drove on toward a town he hadn't visited in decades to bury a man he hadn't spoken to in years.

Despite the time he had been away, the small town of Blackburn looked exactly as it had when Michael was last there, twenty years ago. Perhaps a few more shutters hung crooked, a few more weeds poked through the sidewalk cracks, another shop or two on Main was boarded up, but the place still held a stifling familiarity which made Michael sweat beneath his starched shirt.

He turned left off Main and drove the half-mile to Lone Oak Cemetery. From the road he could see a small white tent set up over what must be his father's grave. Blurry shapes filled the shadows beneath the awning.

As he drove closer, the shapes resolved themselves into discernible things: a few white chairs, even fewer people, and a simple wooden coffin suspended over a dark hole.

Michael stopped his car in the middle of the meandering path, taking a moment to breathe deeply and try his best to prepare for what lay ahead. His eyes roamed over the meager assembly; he did not recognize a single face. The attendees all looked ancient, the few friends his father hadn't outlived.

With two minutes to spare until the funeral officially began, Michael inched his car closer to the burial spot and pulled off to park behind the other vehicles there. Seven heads turned to watch as he unfolded his long legs from the car and stood, smoothing the wrinkles from his clothes and running a hand through his dark hair.

Michael kept his head down as he approached the tent. The last thing he wanted was to catch anyone's eye or draw any more attention to himself than necessary. If he could get out of here without being drawn into conversation with any of his father's old friends, he could be back on the highway and home before dark.

Maybe stop off for a drink on the way.

Michael shook his head to chase away the thought. Diane's disappointed face and weary voice filled his mind again. She'd kill him if he did.

What she doesn't know won't hurt her.

"Ah, you must be his son."

The man's voice took Michael by surprise. He jerked back, startled, as the older gentleman's hand grasped his elbow. Michael caught himself, let out a nervous laugh, made himself stand still.

The man before him was dressed in a dark suit and held a Bible against his chest, marking himself as the preacher – or pastor or priest or whatever it was called – who was responsible for performing the ceremony. Michael didn't know exactly what the man's title was. He certainly didn't know his name. All the arrangements – such as they were – had been planned ahead of time and carried out by his father's lawyer.

Michael shook his head again. The fact that his father had a lawyer at all was a bizarre revelation to him. The man had called three days ago to inform Frank Fenton's only son of his passing. Michael had been four beers into a Sunday afternoon twelve-pack when the call came in. He had listened to the voice coming through the phone, even having the presence of mind to jot down the few details that were passed along, but then he had dropped the notepad to the floor, silenced the phone, turned up the game, and reached for beer number five.

It wasn't until the next day, head pounding and eyes bleary, that Michael had truly registered what the phone call had been about. Diane had found the notepad with his barely legible scribble; she stood in front of him, hands on her hips, demanding loudly – *oh, so loudly* – to know just exactly what was going on.

Now he was here, standing in a gloomy cemetery on an overcast spring day, being stared at by the pastor and the small circle of mourners, wishing he was back on the couch in the den with a cold one in his hand.

Michael cleared his throat, adjusted his tie again.

"Yes. That's me, The – I'm the son. Michael. Michael Fenton."

He extended his hand awkwardly, his eyes focusing just to the side of the pastor's face, avoiding eye contact. The officiant took the hand he offered and shook it slowly and firmly.

"I'm terribly sorry for your loss," he said, and Michael nearly choked on the snort that threatened to explode from his nostrils.

Some loss. If anything, the world was little bit better today for having Frank Fenton gone from it. Michael did not share this thought out loud; instead, he simply nodded and moved toward the rows of chairs. The pastor indicated the seat closest to the casket. Michael was to sit in pride of place, where the eyes of his fellow mourners could bore holes into the back of his head throughout the service.

Yeah, definitely going to need that drink on the way home.

The pastor's words were thankfully few. A scripture read, a hymn stumbled through, a few words about the everlasting peace of the world beyond, then the casket was lowered into the ground.

Michael held his breath as the wooden box rocked back and forth on the straps that held it, his mind for a moment filled with the horrible image of the whole system collapsing and the coffin splintering open as it hit the ground, his father's rotting corpse rolling out onto the grass in front of him.

A few people came around from behind him, picking up clods of earth from the nearby pile – the soil which had been removed to make space for his father's coffin, Michael assumed – and dropping them into the hole.

The dirt made an echoing thud as it hit the top of the wooden box below. Something in the sound made Michael shiver; he folded his long fingers around his bony elbows, waiting for everyone else to leave before he raised his head and stood up.

The pastor still stood there. He gave Michael a slight nod and a sad smile. Michael nodded back, hoping the man would let him pass without speaking. He kept his head down and his eyes on the ground as he walked out from under the tent and toward his vehicle.

Michael's hand was in his pocket, pulling out his keys, when another man stepped around the front of his car. Michael tensed, but the man just smiled and offered his hand as he introduced himself.

"Hello. Mr. Fenton? I'm Jim Brewer, your father's attorney. We spoke on the phone?" The lawyer's voice tilted up into a question at the end as Michael stood staring at him, his own hand still in his pocket.

What the hell did this guy want? If Dad had left him with some massive debts or something, his loan sharks were just going to have to eat their losses.

When it was clear that the younger man wasn't going to simply go away, Michael grudgingly extended his own hand and shook.

"Yeah?" he said, glancing pointedly at his watch. "What do you want?"

The lawyer looked uncertain for a moment before plastering on an unconvincing smile.

"Well, Mr. Fenton, I just need to go over some paperwork with you, some – some things to do with your father's property… you know?"

That goddamn questioning lilt to his voice again. He'd only met the man two minutes ago and already Michael couldn't stand him.

"What paperwork? What property?" Michael's voice came out gruffer than he'd intended, but no matter. Let the little twerp squirm a bit.

"Well, sir, your – your father didn't have much in the way of assets, but there is the house and – and everything in it. It's all yours. I – I have some of the paperwork here, in my car, actually, if – if you'd like to just sign it now. Some of it will have to be notarized, of course, so if you could just stop by the office in the next few days, we can take care of all that. And I – I can give you the keys, uh, if you don't have any of your own."

Michael stared at the lawyer. This was an unexpected complication. It hadn't crossed his mind that he would have to deal with the old man's house.

Probably a drink or two in there. You know how the old bastard loved his liquor.

"Alright, Mr.... Brewer, was it? Get the paperwork. I'll call my wife and tell her I'm going to have a look round the old place and won't be home till morning."

The last twenty years had not been kind to the old Fenton residence. Not that it had ever been a grand sort of place, but Michael's dad used to at least keep the lawn mowed and slap a new coat of paint on the walls every ten years or so.

Now the house seemed to hunch, shrunken into itself, in a yard that was more weeds than grass. Heavy curtains behind all the windows made the glass look black in the evening light. Pale yellow paint had muddied to brown and then faded to gray, peeling in long strips from the wooden siding.

The railing along the front steps left smears of rust like iron bloodstains along Michael's palms as he climbed to the porch. He wiped his hands absentmindedly along his black pants, for once not stopping to worry over what Diane would say. His mind was too focused on the building in front of him to spare a thought for his wife and her nagging.

He hadn't been on this porch, much less inside the house beyond, for half of his lifetime. He'd left at nineteen, eager to make something of himself.

Yeah, and that worked out wonderfully.

His parents had often made the two-hour drive out to Michael's house in the first few years of his marriage to Diane. They had been there to hold their grandchild and attend his first four birthday parties before Mom had died. After that, Dad couldn't be bothered to make the drive on his own.

And you couldn't be bothered to visit him, either.

Michael inserted the key the lawyer had given him into the lock and turned it. The knob was loose in his hand as he twisted it; the door swung inward silently, stopping, half-open, as it snagged on the thick gold carpet that had been in the house longer than Michael had been alive.

Without pushing the door further, Michael squeezed into the narrow opening and twisted himself around the tight space until he was inside.

The whole place stank. Not the eye-watering stench of a rotting corpse – Frank Fenton had at least had the decency to die in the hospital – nor even the smell of long-neglected garbage or greasy dishes left in the sink. No, this was simply the accumulation of smells that spoke of a life lived alone.

The reek of cigarette smoke hung in the air; the once-ivory walls were stained by it. The sweet, yeasty smell of alcohol – likely drinks which had slipped from his father's hands as he drifted into drunken slumber, soaking into the carpet and never being properly cleaned – hovered just below this. The furniture seemed to seep the funk of unwashed bodies, of dirt hiding in folds of flesh, of teeth left unbrushed, skin left unscrubbed. Over it all drifted a nose-tickling trace of ancient dust.

It took a moment for Michael's eyes to adjust to the dimness inside. The thick gold curtains – to match the carpet – blocked out most of the light cast by the setting sun, allowing only a dreamlike glow to permeate the room.

The furniture was the same as it always had been, though a bit more threadbare now than Michael remembered. His father's armchair was pulled directly in front of the old wooden TV cabinet. He could picture the old man sitting there, a drink in one hand, bag of pork rinds in the other, eyes trained on the flickering screen until he nodded off. He wondered how many nights his father had bothered to go to bed at all.

Michael closed the door behind him. There was no overhead light in the living room – for some reason mid-century house designers hadn't seen any need to include them – so he carried on into the kitchen beyond, hand groping along the wall until he found the light switch.

A bare bulb flickered to life, its light steadily brightening until the kitchen at least looked like a half-welcoming place.

Michael looked around.

The old olive-green stove still stood where it always had, a graduated stack of pots and pans sitting on one back burner. His father never put them away in the cabinet; he said, "What's the point, when I'm just going to put them right back on the stove to use them?"

Old plastic Tupperware canisters in earthy colors stood to one side of the chipped sink, a stainless-steel dish rack to the other. Frank Fenton had never installed a dishwasher.

The contents of the dish rack brought an unexpected lump to Michael's throat: one plate, one bowl, one glass, one spoon.

And you know what's in that cabinet right next to the fridge, don't you?

He turned slowly, eyes avoiding the place where his dad kept his liquor.

Not yet.

His gaze fell on the space Michael's mother had called the dining room, though it was less of a room and more of a strange afterthought tacked on, for some reason, to the back end of the kitchen.

It had served well enough as a dining room, he supposed, because there were only three of them. A table pushed directly against the back wall left three short sides available. Michael stopped for a moment to give the knob of the back door – just to the right of the table – a quick turn. Locked. He put his hands to the glass and peered out to the backyard beyond. Only darkness greeted him.

He turned and backtracked through the kitchen (*right there, right there, you know there's some in there*) and living room, stepping this time into the small hallway which contained three doors.

The two doors in front of him stood ajar: his parents' room and the bathroom. The door he had to turn left to see – to his own childhood bedroom – was firmly closed.

Michael stepped into the bathroom, pulled the chain on the bare-bulb light above the sink and mirror. The room was barely large enough to turn around in; Michael instinctively tucked his elbows in close to his body as he entered. Faded green tiles ringed the old tub. No shower here; Dad had never seen the point of installing one. The toilet lid was closed; Michael allowed himself a smile. One small victory for Mom, that was.

A ring of rust marred the curved basin of the sink, and the mirror above showed its age through blackened splotches around the edges, but the bathroom was clean enough.

Michael reached for the latch on the back of the mirror, opening it to reveal the medicine cabinet behind. He half expected to see shelves full of orange prescription bottles for some disease his father had kept secret, but all that greeted him were a few bottles of expired over-the-counter medicines. Aspirin, Benadryl, Pepto. A bent and battered box of Band-Aids stood by itself on the top shelf, yellow with age. No, not alone. Just behind it, poking over the top…

You know just what that is. One of Dad's secret stashes. One of those tiny bottles he nicked from hotel mini-bars. What is it? Vodka? Whiskey? Gin?

Michael closed the mirrored door quickly, snapping the light-chain and taking the two steps required to leave the bathroom as quickly as he could. He pulled the door closed behind him.

His parents' room was nothing more than a black hole yawning before him. A strange, icy frisson traveled up his arms and settled in his shoulders as he looked at it. He didn't know why exactly, but the room felt forbidden, off-limits somehow. It made no sense; he had been allowed in there any time he wanted, growing up.

Well, any time except Thursday nights. But by the time he was old enough to understand why Thursday nights were off-limits, he was old enough to know he wanted to stay as far away from that as possible.

Michael pushed through the odd trepidation and entered the room. Hitting the light switch both illuminated the room and set the ceiling fan to whirring, its steady creaking filling the silence.

Memory hit Michael in the chest like a fist.

Mom had been gone for twelve years now, but nothing in the room had changed in her absence. The flowered bedspread still covered the old mattress, disconcertingly smooth on Mom's side though rumpled on Dad's. An image flashed through Michael's mind: Dad lying perfectly still on his side of the bed every night for twelve years, unwilling to disturb the blankets where his wife had slept. Michael wondered if his mother's pillows would still smell of her perfume, were he to raise one to his nose and sniff.

He didn't want to find out.

Everything was as it should be here, as it had always been: a small pile of change on top of the dresser next to Dad's battered fedora, the mediocre still-lifes Mom had painted in her younger years hanging on the wall, battered paperbacks on each of the bedside tables. Michael leaned closer to look at the book on his mother's side: some dog-eared romance novel with a chiseled hunk on the cover. On Dad's side: last year's *Standard Catalog of Firearms*. Yeah, that seemed about right.

Look lower. In the drawer. You know what's in there. Always a bottle or two. Maybe even a glass if he'd been feeling classy.

Michael stumbled backward out of the room, killing the lights as he went. The ceiling fan made one or two more slow, creaking rotations and stopped. Now only one door remained.

His own room.

He let his hand rest on the doorknob for a moment before turning it. He hadn't been inside the house at all in twenty years, but this room felt like an entire lifetime ago. Had Mom and Dad changed the room at all? Had they ever even stepped foot inside? Would he open the door and find a time-capsule shrine to his adolescent years?

Only one way to find out.

The knob turned stiffly beneath his hand. No one had been in here in a while then – probably at least since Mom died. The door opened into a dark coolness. The smell of smoke and liquor was less in here, though the itch of dust was stronger. Michael's heart pounded in his chest, double time, strong as a bass drum, as he reached in to flip the light on and illuminate the room.

His finger flicked the switch. Nothing happened.

The bulb was burned out. Well, that figured. He was sure his father had never bothered to switch over to the new long-lasting LED bulbs; he probably had a hoard of old-fashioned incandescents out in the garage.

Michael admitted to himself that he was relieved to not have to go into that particular room just yet. He closed the door, a soft click in the silence of the house.

He went into the living room and sat. The nubby upholstery beneath his fingers felt like childhood; he wondered how many Saturday mornings he had lain on this very couch, watching cartoons while his mother fixed breakfast in the kitchen behind him. His father would stumble out of bed hours later, eyes rimmed red and hair sticking up at odd angles, smelling of sour sweat and cheap beer. Michael could hear his mother's voice now, pleading quietly with his father to please not do it again, to please go without it today; he could also hear the clinking of a spoon against the side of his father's mug as he stirred brandy into his coffee.

Hair of the dog, indeed. Yes, the old man had himself a whole kennel-full, didn't he?

Onto Michael's tongue sprang the tart, apple-y sweetness of a bottle of Laird's he had sitting on the mirrored shelf back home. He could picture the bottle in his mind, could see his hand reaching for it.

Except it's not there anymore, is it? Not since Diane went on her cleaning spree.

He had forgotten that.

Fucking teetotaler cunt.

Michael jumped off the couch like he'd touched a live wire. He raked his hands through his hair, making it stand on end. For a moment he seemed to see himself as a blurry image, superimposed over the memory of his father doing the exact same thing.

He shook his head, looked around at the nearly-dark room. The shadows felt as if they might come alive at any moment. He walked until his shins bumped against an end table, then fumbled for the small knob on the table lamp that would bring the relief of at least a little light.

The house was still. Michael walked around, turning on every lamp. He stood in the middle of the room, letting the light pin him in place. Slowly, his heart returned to its normal rhythm.

His stomach growled. Michael laughed at the ridiculousness of it all. He would get out of the house for a few minutes, go grab something to eat down at the diner.

Maybe a little something extra from the liquor store.

Yes, maybe a little something extra, to take the edge off this god-awful day.

Or maybe just raid Dad's old hiding spots. He sure as hell won't be needing the stuff anymore.

No. No, somehow that didn't feel quite right. Not now. Not yet.

Michael pulled up in front of the liquor store ten minutes later, or rather what used to be the liquor store.

Situated at the end of Main in a little, green-roofed building that had always looked a bit out of place, tacked on to the end of the historic brick storefronts that lined most of the street, Blackburn Liquor had been his dad's second home – well, make that his third home, as Philly's Bar was probably the second – for all of Michael's childhood. Now the place was closed, large sheets of plywood nailed up over the windows, faded words painted on the door: *Going Out of Business Sale.*

Well, crap.

Michael pondered driving out of town a bit to Philly's, but there was no telling if that place was still around either, and he really didn't relish the thought of sitting in a crowded bar. Or even an uncrowded bar. He didn't want to be around people, period.

He backed the car out of the parking spot in front of what used to be the liquor store, idling for a moment in the middle of the road. The diner was a couple of blocks down; he could see light spilling from its big front windows onto the sidewalk out front. Most of the businesses along Main closed down at five, but the diner would remain open till eight, if memory served. Michael glanced at the dashboard clock. Just past seven-thirty. He'd better hurry.

Fifteen minutes later, after ordering in a quiet voice and keeping his head down and eyes on the floor while he waited for the food to cook, Michael climbed back into his car with a burger and fries that were already leaking a circle of grease across the bottom of their to-go bag.

He was nearly back to his dad's house when he remembered the Gas-N-Go. A few quick turns took him to the all-night gas station and convenience store. There at the back, in the wall-to-wall glass-fronted refrigerators, sat his salvation. It wasn't the good stuff, wasn't the hard stuff, but it would do.

He returned to his childhood home with a burger and fries and a six-pack of ice-cold Bud.

Michael settled into the dining room, taking his old spot at the table without thinking. He pulled the food from the bag and then flattened it out to use as a plate. The burger and fries disappeared quickly; he barely tasted them, eating only to appease the gnawing in his stomach, hurrying through them to get to the best part of the meal.

He cracked open a bottle, downed the whole thing in three deep gulps.

Then another.

And another.

Michael pushed the last few fries – cold and soggy now – around on their makeshift dish. He felt himself relaxing, the glorious fuzzy buzz of the beer making its way through his bloodstream. He leaned back in his chair, stretched his long legs out beneath the table, and closed his eyes.

The sounds of the house around him were familiar: old wood creaking, the refrigerator humming, a slight scurrying from above that was surely the family of squirrels that had lived in the attic for generations, the distant steady sound of traffic on the highway a few miles off.

"Frank, please don't."

His mother's voice drifted to him, clear but muted, like she was a couple of rooms away. But she wasn't a couple of rooms away, she was right here at the table; Michael knew it, and he knew exactly what his father was about to say in response.

"Marion, a man who works hard all day deserves a cold one with dinner."

"But, Frank…"

"No buts, Marion. I'll do what I want in my own house, and I'll not be nagged about it."

How many times had he heard some version of this conversation play out as they all sat down to dinner? How many times had he watched the exasperation, the disappointment, and the worry play across his mother's face as his father knocked back a beer, then two, then three, in the time it took them to finish their meal?

Well, he was right, though, wasn't he? A man who works hard deserves a little drink at the end of the day. And so does a man who has been through a day as shitty as yours.

Michael opened his eyes. There was truth to that thought, for sure. He balled up the paper sack with the limp fries inside and tossed it into the kitchen garbage can, followed by the three empty bottles.

He opened a fourth and drained it as he stood there, then dropped it in on top of the first three. They made a wonderfully clamorous sound as glass clanged against glass. Michael pulled the last two bottles from their cardboard case, stuck one in the fridge for later, and took the other with him into the living room.

He stared at his dad's chair for a minute, parked right up in front of the television. Not able to bring himself to sit in it, he grunted and strained as he shifted it instead, moving it back to the position it had always held when he was growing up. This cleared his view of the TV, so he grabbed the remote and sat down ungracefully, the couch's old brown cushions rising up to meet him.

He hit the power button, then flinched as the TV came to life at full volume, a man's voice shouting in Michael's ear. He squinted against the sound, finally opening one eye in order to find the button on the remote which would turn it down. The image on the screen was of an older man in an ugly suit standing behind a wooden pulpit on a massive stage.

"Oh, Christ, Dad, really? Late night televangelists?"

A quick flick through the channels revealed nothing of any interest, but that was okay because Michael was now more than halfway through his fifth beer and was happy to simply scrunch a throw pillow up against the armrest, pull the blanket which lay folded across the back of the couch down over his body, and lay back, letting the alcohol take him to that wonderfully happy place where he just didn't give a shit about much of anything.

He fell asleep to the droning voice of the anchor on the nine o'clock news.

"What the hell does a man have to do to get some peace and quiet around here?"

Michael stirred at the words, shifting his body so that he faced the back of the couch, pulling his arms and legs up into a tight ball on the narrow cushions.

"Shut that kid up or I'll give him something to really cry about!"

The voice was distant, echoing, at once strangely distorted and yet intimately familiar. Michael pulled the edges of the pillow down around his head, trying to cover his ears and block out the sound. He was deep enough into his inebriated slumber that if he could just silence the noise, he could fall right back to sleep.

"Well, what do we have here? A sleeping beauty?"

The voice was closer this time, close enough to send prickles of warning down the skin of Michael's arms. He jerked and twisted in one ungraceful movement, ending on his back with his eyes wide open.

He stared into the leering face of his father.

Thin wisps of graying hair stretched across the old man's splotched scalp. Redness ringed his watery eyes and a few drops of spittle dotted his stubbled chin. He grinned at Michael; yellowed teeth set in pale gums behind bloodless lips.

Michael sat up quickly, stiffly, pulling his thin blanket against him like a child invoking protection against some underbed bogeyman.

The old man laughed, a hoarse yet liquid sound, thick phlegm passing over parched vocal cords. He straightened up, hands on his hips, staring down at his son. Then he walked over to his old armchair and sat down heavily, the chair's springs creaking in protest which did not match the weight of the old man's small and wasted body.

Michael forced himself to breathe, slowly, in and out, in and out. This couldn't be real. This had to be a dream. He slid one hand along the opposite arm, trying not to draw attention to the movement.

He pinched himself, hard.

Nothing happened except for a smarting pain in his arm where his fingernails had dug into the skin.

"What's the matter, son? No words of greeting for your old man? Cat got your tongue?"

Frank Fenton leaned back in his chair, kicking the footrest up as he cracked open a can of Busch that hadn't been in his hand a moment before.

Michael simply stared, open-mouthed and speechless, at his dead father.

"No matter. You never were much of a conversationalist, anyway. We'll just see what's on the tube."

The old man threw his head back, drained the can in one long gulp. Streams of beer flowed out from the corners of his mouth and down his chin, soaking into the fabric of his checkered shirt. He dropped the can on the floor next to him. It landed with a clatter on a pile of other empties, twenty at least.

Michael looked at the small pyramid. A few of the cans still dripped beer, a trickling waterfall of waste. He rubbed his eyes. Those cans had not been there before. How long had he been asleep? How long had his father – his dead father – been in the room with him, how long had he been drinking?

Oh, God. How drunk was the old man? Was it enough to...

His father's rough hand caught Michael against his left temple with a slap hard enough to knock his head sideways and send his brain pinballing inside his skull.

"Hey! What the hell was that for?" Michael was halfway out of his seat before he realized that his father still sat in the old recliner, eyes glued to the TV screen. Michael lifted a hand to his head. The spot was tender. But there was no way, no way the old man could have walloped him and gotten back into his chair that fast.

Michael's head pounded and his vision swam. He sat back down on the couch, put his face in his hands and willed himself to breathe. He just needed to breathe, just needed to count to ten – maybe make that a hundred, needed to let his brain settle for a moment, and then when he looked up again, he would be alone in the living room, alone in the flickering light of the television.

One.

Two.

Three.

He made it to twenty-four before he heard the voice.

"Frank, honey, please. No more tonight."

Michael's breath caught in his throat. He peeked through his fingers. His mother, young and beautiful but already looking tired and careworn, stood in the doorway leading to the kitchen. His father – young again now, too, stronger, less stooped, hair still thick on top of his head – stood in front of her.

Marion Fenton tried to block the doorway with her slight frame, tried to keep her husband from going into the kitchen. Michael knew why. He had watched this scene unfold a thousand times growing up.

"Out of the way, Marion."

Frank Fenton moved toward his wife. He towered over her. She did not back down. She put one hand on his chest, cupped his cheek with the other.

"Frank, baby, please."

Michael flinched and covered his eyes again. He knew what was coming a split second before it came. The sharp sound of an open palm meeting the soft flesh of a woman's face. His mother cried out, stumbled back. His father's footsteps entered the kitchen, work boots clomping against the linoleum.

The sound of the refrigerator opening, closing again. The crack and hiss of a can opening.

Michael dared to look again. His mother stood with her back against the doorway, her hands up to hold the spot on her cheek where a bruise blossomed against her skin. His father stalked past her without glancing in her direction, walked back toward his...

But his father was already in the chair. *Still* in the chair. He was old and bent and the pile of cans next to him was as tall as the armrests now, glass bottles mixed in with the cans, all of it dripping onto the gold carpet, a boozy stain spreading below.

Michael glanced back toward the kitchen doorway. It was empty.

He bent forward, head between his knees now, counting again.

Twenty-five.

Twenty-six.

Twenty-seven.

At sixty-eight he heard the unmistakable sound of the back door opening and then slamming shut. A child's running footsteps. A peal of laughter that broke his heart with its innocence. A shout of childish joy.

"What the hell are you so damn happy about? And why are you inside? I told you to go outside and play."

The footsteps came to an abrupt halt, small sneakers skidding to a stop on the shag carpet.

"Daddy?"

Michael sucked in a sharp breath of air. His arms shook as he lowered them; his head felt like lead as he lifted it to see the boy who stood in the middle of the room.

Blue polyester shorts, a grass-stained white T-shirt, knee-high socks with red stripes around the top, dirty shoes. A mop of brown hair in need of cutting, green eyes bright in a sweaty face, a tentative smile as the child approached the man in the chair, holding something in his hands.

What was it? What had he found that day? A frog? A lizard? An especially long worm? Michael couldn't remember. But he knew this scene, knew this day, knew this memory though it had been long buried in the darkest corner of his mind.

He knew what would happen next.

"Marion!" His father's voice was loud enough to echo off the walls. "Where the hell are you? Come deal with this kid!"

The boy approached his father, small hands with their mysterious offering still held out in supplication.

"Daddy, Mama's not here. She's gone to the store, remember?"

The man glared at the child.

"Not here, hmmm? The store? Yeah. Well, get on outside till she gets back, kid. Your old dad is resting."

"But, Daddy," the child said, hope and fear mixed in his voice, and Michael in his adult form wished for nothing more than to be able to reach out and snatch the boy away from what he knew was coming.

His father was up and out of his chair in a flash. The man's strong hands wrapped around the boy's upper arms, lifted him from the ground, and threw him. The boy landed against the heavy coffee table, his left thigh hitting the hard edge of the wood with a sickening crack. He let out a single startled cry of pain, then curled up on the floor, arms wrapped around his knees, the bones of his left leg pushing oddly against the skin.

Michael remembered it all too clearly. His father had fallen back into his chair, downed the last of his drink, and had been snoring softly, his head forward against his chest, when Michael's mother came home from doing the weekly grocery shopping.

She had rushed her son to the hospital.

Michael had spent the rest of his sixth summer hobbling around, his leg in a cast, his eyes focused downward, his childlike innocence forever marred.

He dropped his head back between his knees now, swallowed hard against the bile that rose in his throat.

Sixty-nine.

Seventy.

But there, in between seventy-one and seventy-two, a small sob.

"What now?" Michael spoke the thought aloud, a frightened and hopeless whisper. He held perfectly still, not counting but not looking either. A few moments of silence passed. Maybe he had imagined the sound.

But then it came again.

A quiet hiccupping cry, a sniffle, the sound of someone shifting.

The *feel* of someone shifting. On the couch. Right next to him.

Michael lifted his head. Let his vision slide slowly to the right. A form sharpened into existence beside him. A small form. What now? Some other god-forsaken memory from his childhood come back to torment him?

But, no.

The child was so small that his legs just reached the edge of the cushions, feet sticking out straight over the empty air below.

Michael's eyes focused. He concentrated on the shoes. They lit up, red flashes against the darkness every time the child shifted.

He never had shoes like that.

But Nathan did.

A new level of fear gripped Michael's heart as his eyes traveled upward, along the child's legs and torso, finally stopping to look into the tear-stained face of his own son.

"Nathan, Nathan, buddy, what's wrong?" Michael's voice sounded strange and echoing in his ears.

The child looked up at him, but no, that wasn't quite right. He looked *through* him. Michael turned, suddenly afraid of what he would find, of what his son saw behind him.

The room was shadowy. A television continued to flicker but it wasn't his dad's old wooden console, it was a sleek black plastic thing set on a shelf made of steel and glass.

The walls were pushed back, distant, the TV's light illuminating only a small patch of a much larger room. Columns rose up into what seemed an impossible distance. Michael's hands gripped the couch beneath him, but beneath his fingers the upholstery was no longer the old, nubby knit of his parents' furniture but the sleek gray leather of his own couch, in his own basement.

Michael's fingers touched something else. A hand.

His own hand.

He jumped off the couch, a strangled cry forcing its way from his throat.

He stood in the middle of the room.

He stared at himself, a decade younger.

The man on the couch – *that's me, that's me* – was out cold. One hand rested across his chest, the other hung straight out, a bottle dangling from the loose fingertips.

The little boy – *my little boy, my son* – sat at the man's feet, sniffling quietly. The child seemed to gather his resolve. He rose to his knees – *again, he's done it before, countless times* – and grasped his sleeping father's feet, shaking them, gently at first, then more roughly.

"Daddy! Daddy, wake up! Please wake up, Daddy!"

The man on the couch let out an enormous snorting snore, scratched at his chin with his free hand. Then the hand dropped back to his chest. He slept on.

The child – *Nathan, my Nathan* – dropped back against the cushions. He raised his knees, crossed his arms atop them, bent his head into the small dark space this created, and cried.

Michael was filled with a sudden fury. He rushed toward the man on the couch *(his self, himself)*, meaning to shake him, to jolt him awake, to make him look at his poor son *(our son, my son, my boy)*, but his hands went right through him. Michael's momentum carried him forward; he fell, headfirst, onto the couch, spinning, lost in a vortex of darkness, his body stretching, mind screaming until –

He startled awake.

He lay on the couch, the good old nubby couch, his neck cricked at a horrible angle against the armrest. Michael stayed still for a few moments, staring at the back of the couch, his heart rate slowly coming back to something resembling normalcy.

The TV screen threw gray light over the wall behind him, the static white noise of a station off the air a strange comfort to him.

But something… something wasn't right. As Michael's mind sharpened into wakefulness, two thoughts came to the forefront. The first: stations didn't go off the air anymore. The second: he had gone to sleep with all the living room lamps, plus the kitchen and hall lights, still on; the room was now dark except for the TV's glow.

A lurching feeling kicked him hard in the stomach. Ice seemed to form along every inch of exposed skin as he heard the sound.

A cry. A sob. A whimper.

But not that of a child this time.

This was the sound of an old man weeping.

Michael turned himself over slowly, carefully, hoping that the couch would not creak beneath his weight as he moved.

There, in the old armchair, sat his father. The man was diminished, frail, his once-thinning hair now gone, leaving nothing but a shining pate marked with liver spots. He wore old pajamas, several sizes too big. His arm shook as he raised a bottle to his lips.

Michael recoiled in horror at the contents of the bottle. The liquid inside was black, viscous. When his father drank it, the alcohol – for that was surely what it was, though some strange and sickening vintage that Michael had never known – glugged and gurgled in the bottle's neck, as though something solid blocked the way.

The old man took no notice of Michael. He drank and cried, swallowed and sobbed, whispered and mumbled. Michael had the impression that the man was struggling against something, begging, pleading; he realized after a time that it was the bottle itself that his father was fighting, the bottle which never seemed to become any less full no matter how much the man drank.

A pang of pity worked its way into Michael's heart. His father was a mean old bastard, but Michael understood all too well the battle he was facing, the constant pull of the truest friend and worst enemy man could know, the seductive allure of the bottle.

He stood up, legs shaking beneath him. It took only three steps to cross the room. Michael knelt next to his father's chair, reached toward the old man, touched him gently on the thin arm which held the cursed drink.

The old man froze. The tremors which shook his body lessened until they stopped completely. His sobs faded into heaving breaths and then into the slow and steady rise of his sunken chest. The hand that gripped the bottle tightened, the skin blanching white around the knuckles.

Frank Fenton began to laugh. A low, crackling rumble filled his body, rising to high, maniacal peaks as it exploded from his mouth.

Michael held his breath.

The old man's head began to rise and turn.

Michael let go of his father's arm. He rocked back quickly, putting distance between himself and the sight before him.

Frank Fenton was changed.

His skin was sunken, clinging to bones which protruded almost to the point of breaking through the flesh. His eyes were nothing more than dark chasms. Lips stained with the vile drink pulled back into a rictus grin, showing toothless gums. His laughter filled the room, rising and reverberating around the old, paneled walls.

He laughed until Michael thought he would go mad with the sound, until Michael pressed both hands over his ears to block it out.

He laughed until he choked, and as he gagged, out of Frank Fenton's mouth rushed a stream of muddy ooze, a dark waterfall of rot and ruin and booze. The stench of it hit Michael with a force that knocked him backward, hands planting on the floor behind him to keep from falling flat.

The carpet was wet, slimy and saturated. The reek of fermentation rose to Michael's nostrils, the rancid smell of a thousand spilled drinks. The wetness soaked into his pants, squished between his bare toes, permeated the skin of his palms until he felt that he was sinking in a flood of alcohol. He tried to move, to crab-walk backward, to climb up onto the safety of the couch, but his hands and feet slipped in the liquid, his body sinking deeper, the soaked carpet swallowing him like quicksand.

Bony hands reached toward him, gripped his face. His father was climbing over the side of the chair, his body twisted impossibly, his arms grown horrifically long, ribs spreading until his torso looked segmented, flesh pale and bloated like a maguey worm. Michael panicked, thrashing, but the thing that had been his father held his head firmly in its grip.

"You can't get away, boy, you'll never get away. Have a drink, boy, have a drink. Drink!"

The father-creature cradled Michael's head in the crook of one arm and brought the bottle of black sludge to his mouth. Michael pressed his lips together firmly, turning his head from side to side as much as he could. The bottle rim pressed against his mouth, the fluid inside it alive, wriggling against his lips, trying to gain entry.

Michael closed his eyes, closed them against the horrid sight of his father's face, against the heady reek of the alcohol, against the sound of the laughter which still echoed around the room. He lifted his hands, grasping his father's insectile arms and pushing against them.

The bottle ground against his lips, hard against his teeth. He tasted blood as the glass rim broke through the skin, and then the coppery taste was joined with something else, something far worse, something awful yet unavoidable.

Michael jerked his head again, breaking free for a moment from the relentless pressure of the bottle. His mouth opened, gasping for breath.

"No!" he shouted, and the word repeated inside his head.

No! No! No!

Stop! Stop!

"No! Stop! Please!"

The voice was not his own.

Michael opened his eyes, and the room spun. He was no longer on the floor. He sat in his father's chair, turned sideways. His hands did not grip the skeletal arms of his father.

They gripped the arms of his son.

Nathan cowered on the floor beside him, arms up defensively, head turned away from his father, from Michael. Tears streamed down the teenager's face as he begged.

"No! Stop! Please!"

No. No. Stop. Please.

Michael mumbled in his sleep on the old brown couch. His mind struggled to swim its way through the sea of drunken slumber, to find its way to consciousness. With a gasping breath he broke through. He sat up, arms flailing, incoherent words still spilling from his mouth.

~ 161 ~

He swung around, planted his feet on the floor. His body was tense, braced for a fight, but he shook all over. The room swam circles around him when he stood, his legs too unsteady to hold him. He fell back onto the couch, trembling.

The room slowly stopped its revolutions. His heartbeat calmed, calmed, calmed until he could breathe again.

All the lights were on. Every lamp in the living room burned, the bare bulbs overhead in the kitchen and hallway shone out their welcome glow. The TV was on, some late-night infomercial for cleaning products.

Michael put his head in his hands and began to laugh.

The laughter turned to tears.

The tears turned to sobs.

The sobs turned to screams.

You need a drink.

Michael looked up. His head turned toward the kitchen. There was one last beer, sitting cold and ready for him in the fridge.

You need something a little harder than beer this time, don't you think?

Michael sat for a moment, his brain numb but his body craving, crying out for that gift which would make it all go away.

Hair of the dog, boy. Hair of the dog.

He stood. The room only spun a couple of times before righting itself.

Michael made his way into the kitchen.

He stood before his father's liquor cabinet.

He opened the door.

It was empty.

"Fuck."

It's okay. You know all his hiding spots. There has to be something somewhere.

Michael made his way through the house. He checked all the places.

Behind the boxes in the top of the hall closet.

In the drawer of Dad's bedside table.

The bathroom medicine cabinet.

Behind the Band-Aids! An ancient bottle of mouthwash? Fuck!

Michael grew more frantic with each passing second, more desperate, more angry.

Inside the tall vase on the hallway bookshelf.

Under the grill that used to house the floor furnace.

There has to be something somewhere. Find it. Fast. Whiskey. Gin. Doesn't matter. Some fucking wine, for God's sake. We need it now. Find it. Find something. Tequila. Rum. Vodka.

Vodka!

The freezer.

Michael rushed to the kitchen, pulled the freezer door open with such force that the entire refrigerator rocked.

A couple of TV dinners. Some unidentifiable meat covered in frost. A carton of ice cream. No vodka.

Michael grabbed the ice cream and threw it across the room, letting loose a roar of desperate rage. The carton hit the door to the garage and fell like a brick to the floor below.

The garage.

Michael kicked the ice cream out of the way and yanked open the garage door. He palmed the inner wall until he hit the light switch.

Dad's car took up most of the space. Two large mechanic's toolboxes sat flush against one wall; above them were crude wooden shelves stacked neatly with cleaning supplies, motor oil, lawn chemicals, household supplies.

Michael's eyes roved over the shelves. He yanked open every drawer in the toolboxes, the metal tools clanging against each other in an ear-splitting racket.

He checked inside the car, under the seats, in the trunk.

Nothing.

Not a single goddamned ounce of liquor in the whole goddamned house.

Michael turned and swept his arm across the loaded shelves, sending bottles and cans and boxes tumbling to the ground.

He looked around once more, tears in his eyes, a whimpering sob working its way up from his chest. His eyes fell on a stack of boxes. G&E 60-watt bulbs.

My bedroom.

Grabbing one of the boxes, ripping it open as he walked, Michael made his way back through the house, through the kitchen, the living room, the hall. He charged into his old room, using the dim illumination from the hallway to guide him as he changed out the decades-old bulb for a new one. He flipped the switch.

The room came to life.

For a moment, Michael Fenton forgot about his search.

The room was exactly as he had left it, twenty years ago. His old twin bed, covered in its blue and red quilt, sat in the corner. His desk, right next to the bed, still held his green library lamp, his stack of paperbacks, the scored scars of teenage boredom.

Tacked up on the wall, the band posters and bikini-clad models looked as fresh as the day he'd hung them. Through the closet door, left slightly ajar, he could see a row of empty hangers and the few articles of clothing he had not taken with him when he moved out.

A wave of dizziness that had nothing to do with his inebriation and everything to do with the overpowering nostalgia which gripped him spun the world around. Michael's ears were filled with the pounding of his heartbeat and a rushing ocean of pulsing blood. He thought for a moment that his heart had actually stopped, his lungs ceased their inhalations.

Time stood still.

Michael stood in the center of the room and watched as a thousand memories played out, himself at five, at twelve, at sixteen, images moving around him like multiple old films superimposed one over another over another.

God, how much of his life had been spent in this room? Holed up, hiding, steering clear of his father, of his parents' fights, of the smell of booze and the tension which reigned whenever Dad was home. He was always in here, in this room, in his little sanctuary, his prison. Always alone.

Just like Nathan.

Oh, God, just like Nathan.

Nathan is fine. He's just a moody teenager. He'll be fine. You were fine. You are fine.

No. No, he wasn't fine. He wasn't fine at all.

You just need a drink. A drink will fix it. A drink will make it better. Will make it go away. You'll be fine. Nathan is fine. You're fine. Just. Need. A. Drink.

There was no alcohol here. No bottles hidden in his old room. He didn't have to look, didn't have to tear things apart, didn't have to disturb the sanctity of this haven. He simply knew.

But there's a bottle in the fridge. A good cold Bud. Not the hard stuff, no, but better than nothing. In the fridge. In the kitchen. Just turn around and walk through the house. Grab the bottle. Everything will be fine.

Michael stood still, rooted to the spot, rooted to his past, rooted to his pain.

He saw it then. A white envelope against the white pillowcase. A single word on the front: MIKE.

Michael stumbled toward the bed, grabbed the envelope, sat down.

He cursed his clumsy fingers as he fumbled the envelope open. Inside was a single sheet of notebook paper, covered in writing.

Mike,

My boy. This is the hardest letter I'll have to write, the hardest apology to make, and I still don't know if I'll ever have the guts to actually mail this off, but Step 9 says I have to at least try to make amends. I was wrong, son. I was horribly, horribly wrong. I did you wrong, did your mother wrong, for all those years. I have no excuse. I have a reason. I was addicted. A drunk of the highest caliber. But a reason is not an excuse, because it doesn't excuse the things I did. The way I acted. The way I treated your mother. And you. I'm so sorry. I ruined all of our lives. I see that the demon has made its way into your blood, too, Mike. I see that you're following in your old man's footsteps. I hope you can find help, son. I hope that I haven't ruined you completely. I know that I put you through so much. Too much. I know it might be too late for us. I ask for your forgiveness but more than that I ask that you look at yourself and make your own changes before it's too late for you, too. For you and your son. For Nathan. I love you, son, though I know I never really showed it. But I do. I love you. And... that's all. I'll probably never work up the nerve to send this anyway, but I love you.

Dad

Michael sat for a long time, staring at the letter.

Dad had... cleaned up? Gone sober? Suddenly the TV preacher made a certain sense. But why? How? When? There was no date on the letter. Why hadn't Dad sent it?

Well, hell, Michael could answer that one.

It was too damn hard.

He thought about his father, and he thought about his mother. He thought about himself, his wife, his own marriage.

Then Michael Fenton thought about his son, and he wept. He lay down on his childhood bed, in his childhood home, and he wept bitter tears until exhaustion took him and he slept, curled up on the blue and red quilt, the letter, damp with tears, slowly falling from his hand as his grip loosened.

It was nearly eleven in the morning when Michael woke. The distant sound of his ringing phone brought him slowly out of the dark void of sleep to the light of day.

He lay for a while, stretching slowly, forcing blood back into his cramped limbs. He looked around the room, his room, and his heart filled with both a fondness and an ache for this place where he had spent his growing-up years.

Eventually, the phone began to ring again. Michael's head pounded as he walked to the living room and fished around between the couch cushions until he found it. He had just missed the call.

Diane.

She had called half a dozen times, though she had left no messages.

She was probably mad as hell. Well, she had a right.

He wasn't quite ready to talk to her yet, so he sent off a text instead: **Sorry. I was asleep. Been a long night. But I'm OK. Going to finish up a few things here before I head home.**

Michael hit SEND. He stared at the screen for a moment before typing three more words and adding them to the message.

I love you.

He didn't really have anything to finish up at his father's house, but he needed time to sit with his thoughts. With his memories. With his pain.

With the harsh truth.

The sun rose high in the sky outside. Its rays made their way in around the edges of the curtains, and Michael's eyes ached at the brightness. He got some aspirin from the bathroom, washed it down with glass after glass of water from the kitchen sink. His stomach growled, and he wondered if it was safe now to eat something, if it would stay down if he did.

Best solution to this problem is some hair of the dog.

The words repeated in his mind as he thought about the one remaining bottle in the refrigerator.

hair of the dog hair of the dog hair of the dog

One of his father's favorite phrases, that. Just need a little hair of the dog, and everything is fine.

Michael opened the fridge. The bottle stood by itself on a shelf.

He picked it up, walked to the table, set it down.

He sat down, not in his own spot, but in the place that had always been reserved for his father.

He stared at the bottle, stared until the glass began to sweat, until the puddled ring around the bottom had spread an inch all the way round.

He picked the bottle up, walked to the counter, popped the lid off.

He poured it down the sink, and ran water after it for five minutes just to make sure no traces remained.

He dropped the bottle in the trash, then tied up the bag and walked it out to the metal cans outside.

Michael walked through the house, turning off lights, taking one last long look around before locking the door behind him as he left.

He stopped at the diner for a late lunch, which he planned to eat in the car as he drove. Before he pulled out of the parking lot, he checked his phone. A message from Diane had come through.

It simply said: **I love you, too.**

God, the things that woman had put up with through the years. She was a saint, truly. And Nathan... oh, Nathan.

Michael took a few deep breaths. He had cried enough for the day, and would surely cry more later, but right now he needed to drive. He thumbed through his phone's directory, found Diane's name, hit CALL.

It went to voicemail, which he couldn't pretend to be surprised about, but he left a message anyway.

"Hey, baby. I'm heading home now, should be there in a couple of hours if traffic isn't too crazy. Had a rough night. Did a lot of thinking. Can't – can't wait to get home to you, and to Nathan. Maybe we can do something together, the three of us, when I get back? And then – then we need to have a talk. And I – I need to do some things. To work on some things. I – I'll explain later. But I love you. And I love Nathan. Tell him for me, would you? I – I'll be home soon. Bye."

Michael drove down Main Street, out of Blackburn, onto the highway.

He definitely had some things to work on. And the house – Dad's house – to deal with as well. They'd need to clean it out, maybe fix it up a bit, put it on the market. Maybe that was something he and Nathan could do together, a project that would take a few months' worth of weekends. Maybe they could talk while they worked.

Talking was always easier when your hands had something to keep them busy at the same time.

Yeah. He and Nathan. They had some things to talk about.

Now, before it was too late.

THE VEIL

The sunset through my bedroom window
Paints fiery-orange light,
Dappled with the fluttering shadows
Of a thousand not-yet-fallen leaves
Against a gray wall.

Fire against the dark,
Like a soul's last triumphant spark
As it flees this mortal coil.

The veil grows thin this time of year –
Or so they say –
Allowing contact between the spirits
Shuffled off, and the souls still
Here, bound in flesh.

Voices in the dark –
A call across an eternal chasm,
Reaching through the night.

Echoes of the Dead

The stories outline specters dire and dim:
Revenants, shades,
Remnants of life, deluded, denied,
Come back to seek revenge
And inspire fear.

But alone in the dark,
The people of the old ways
Know better, and seek wisdom.

What would I not give, in truth,
For the outline of my mother to appear,
My grandmother's pale form draw near,
To let loose this torment of words and tears
That only they would understand?

I wait, silent, in the dark:
Breath held, head bowed,
And wish the veil so thin I could fall through.

DECISIONS
A True Tale

The previous stories in this book are obvious works of fiction. The final entry in this collection is truth. Fact. Memoir, if you will. It is my own story. And a little bit my mother's. So far in this book, you've read some psychological horror and some grief horror; both are also included here, in the realest and rawest of ways. While the stories that came before this contain a balance of good and bad endings, this one, the real one, contains a little of both, but in the end...

Well, I'll let you read and find out.

I've had a few brushes with death in my life. When I was eight years old, my grandfather died (liver/lung cancer). At ten, my great-grandmother died (she was old and it was simply her time). Two days before my thirteenth birthday, my Grandma Virginia passed (brain cancer). In January of 2006, on my daughter Rebecca's fourth birthday, my Grandma Nan died in her sleep (again, she was old and it was her time).

I missed my Grandma Nan immensely. We were incredibly close. We had similar personalities: exceptionally intelligent and observant, lovers of dark, macabre literature and movies, dry and sometimes dirty senses of humor. During my pre-teen and early teen years, we often butted heads. Two smart, strong, opinionated, and relentlessly stubborn women in the same space tends to end that way. Grandma Nan was fond of saying that I'd argue with a stop sign if I'd put it in place myself.

Which was true. But also true: she'd do the same thing.

Sometime around my sixteenth birthday, I realized that the reason we clashed so spectacularly was because we were so much alike. And then I realized that instead of running up against each other all the time, we could be each other's best friends and co-conspirators. And we were. For the next nine years, we grew wonderfully close. We discussed books and movies and poetry and men and children and everything else you could think of.

Once I was married and living on my own, I called my grandma at least a couple of times each week to talk. Sometimes we'd chat for ten minutes, sometimes for an hour.

She was my confidante, my advice-giver, my listening ear and shoulder to cry on.

After she passed, it took me months to get used to her being gone, months before I stopped thinking of something important or funny and immediately reaching for the phone to call and talk to her about it.

Almost five years later, when my fourth pregnancy (after three healthy babies) ended in miscarriage, I missed her all over again. Sitting alone in the bathroom, bleeding and crying, I would have given anything to talk to someone who had been through what I was experiencing – Grandma Nan had suffered four miscarriages and one stillbirth in addition to her two healthy babies.

But the most recent death I've been close to was my own mother's. And that is what this story is about.

I feel like I should preface this section with the fact that I loved my mother immensely. She was a good mom. She made my childhood magical, and once I reached adulthood, she was always willing to give me whatever help she could.

I'm going to say a lot of things in the next few pages which sound like I'm talking badly about her. I mean no ill intent toward her or her memory, but there comes a time when we have to face the truth of who our parents are – the good and the bad – and to realize that we love them in spite of the actions and decisions they made in their own lives that we disagree with or can't understand. And most of all, there comes a time when we realize we can learn from their mistakes.

My mother was diagnosed with stage three colo-rectal cancer early in 2011. I was pregnant at the time – having conceived again just two months after the aforementioned miscarriage. She went through chemo and radiation – but the doctors warned us that I, as a pregnant woman, should not be around her while she was having the radiation treatments as the residual radiation could harm the growing baby.

When my son, Andrew, was born in September of that year, my mother was having the cancer – and quite a bit of her inner workings – cut out. We were on different floors of the same hospital. During recovery, she contracted MRSA.

She wasn't able to see her new grandson until he was several weeks old.

She persevered.

My mother would live for another eleven years.

She would never be quite the same, though.

Her mental health had never been great; she'd been through a number of therapists and psychologists and psychiatrists and diagnoses and treatments and medications in the fifteen years or so before they discovered the cancer. Dealing with a potentially terminal illness did nothing to improve this.

Although she was eventually declared cancer-free, her body never truly recovered. She was physically weak and highly susceptible to germs and illness.

She lived with my brother and his family for a while. She lived with us for a while. She remarried a man I begged her not to marry (more on that later) and lived with him for a while – up until the point that neither of them could properly care for themselves or each other.

They moved in with me, for the last time, in May of 2021.

My husband (now my ex) and I had just bought a huge old house in a small town in Oklahoma. We all lived together there – myself, my husband, our four youngest kids, and my mom and her husband, for fifteen months.

Some of my favorite memories with my mother are the many warm, lazy afternoons we spent sitting in the rocking chairs on my front porch, just talking. Recalling old memories, discussing books and movies, telling jokes, singing songs, and sometimes delving deep into serious and oftentimes sad subjects.

In August of 2022, my daughter Rebecca, who was still living at home (though preparing for her wedding) came down with Covid. She worked as a phlebotomist at one of the large local hospitals; it seemed only a matter of time before she contracted the illness. As soon as she found out, she quarantined herself, but by that point, it was too late. Eight people in one house. The inevitable happened.

I immediately quarantined Mom and her husband to their own room in the hopes of sparing them from the sickness. I ordered in masks and gloves and tests and medication and cans of Lysol and multiple boxes of Clorox wipes.

It happened anyway. Everyone got it. Some were barely sick at all – Rebecca was recovered and back to work in practically no time, the younger kids had two or three days of sniffly noses and upset tummies and then bounced back. My husband never even took a day off work. My teenage son had pretty cruddy cold symptoms for a week or so.

Mom's husband coughed a lot but seemed otherwise okay. He, being older and considered high-risk, was given a prescription to take, which probably helped.

Mom was given the same prescription. Thank God I took the time to read the package insert before I gave it to her. People with compromised hepatic systems (kidneys that don't function properly) were specifically warned NOT to take the medication. I called my mom's home health nurse to ask about it, and she gave me an emphatic NO DON'T GIVE IT TO HER!

So, Mom suffered along, un-medicated, with the rest of us.

How was I?

I was the sickest of all.

I was constantly lightheaded. Nauseated. I had to sit down halfway up the stairs because my vision would start to go black around the edges from just that exertion. Eventually, when I couldn't make it across the house without my knees buckling and the room spinning, my husband took me to the ER.

I was severely dehydrated, and quite honestly, exhausted.

They told me to go home, drink lots of water, and stay in bed for a few days.

Obviously they had never been the one person responsible for taking care of seven other people. I couldn't stay in bed for an hour without someone needing me, let alone days.

My mother needed me most of all. For several months leading up to this point, her health and strength had been deteriorating rapidly. She couldn't walk on her own; she had to use a walker. Often, she couldn't even use that and I had to half-carry her from her bed to her chair or to the bathroom and back. She had developed a problem with her stoma site. I will spare you the details, but suffice it to say that it involved lots of blood and many trips to the emergency room.

She had been on home health care for a couple of months before we all contracted Covid. She barely ate. She was constantly on the cusp of dehydration no matter what we did. Her blood pressure remained disturbingly low. She had zero strength. She forgot things a lot and was often confused. It was like she dreamed things and then was convinced that they had really happened.

She was diagnosed with non-alcoholic cirrhosis of the liver; several times she was admitted to the hospital to have fluid drained from her abdomen. Her kidneys began to have decreased function as well.

She was not healthy, and she hadn't been for a long time.

Those last few days, before they took her to the hospital for the final time, are a blur of my own sickness and misery mixed with caring for my mother. She would call for me, and I would drag myself off the couch and stumble into her room to lift her out of bed and attempt to keep us both upright all the way to the bathroom. I don't know how many times I had to kneel there in her bathroom floor, holding onto the cabinet for dear life, my own vision swimming in and out of focus, my body flushing with fever, fighting to stay conscious long enough to get her back to bed.

Eventually, I did start to feel better.

Mom didn't.

It wasn't the Covid itself. She wasn't having cold-like symptoms. It was the way the Covid drained her body of its already-depleted resources and exacerbated all her other medical problems.

Then came the day they took her.

I had managed to get her to the bathroom. Her stoma was bleeding profusely; it literally painted the bathroom floor and walls with blood. It was worse than I had ever seen before, and it had been really bad many times in the past. I took a video and sent it to her home health nurse. She told me to call 911 immediately.

The EMTs in our small town were already quite familiar with us by this point; Mom had been to the ER in Tulsa, an hour away, via ambulance at least half a dozen times already.

But this time was different. This time they walked in, saw the blood, saw that Mom could not hold herself up at all, and called for Life Flight.

They loaded her into the back of the ambulance and drove her to our small local hospital to wait for the helicopter.

Before they rolled her out my front door, she turned to us and said, "I won't be coming back this time."

A condensed version of my memories of the next two weeks goes something like this…

After two or three days, when I was finally cleared to go out and about among the masses, my daughter Rebecca and I drove into Tulsa to visit Mom at the hospital. Up to this point, I had received piecemeal bits of information from phone calls. Trying to talk to Mom herself on the phone was useless; half the time she either couldn't find her phone when it rang or didn't know it was ringing at all, and when she did answer, her words were slurred and she would trail off in the middle of sentences. I talked to her nurse at least once a day, though, and the nurse assured me that while Mom was "out of it" mentally, she was in no real danger.

When we went up to visit her, Mom was in a Covid isolation room. We had to pass through multiple doors, scrubbing in before entering. We were supposed to wear masks as well, but when we informed the nurses that we had already had the exact same strain of Covid that Mom had, they let us take the masks off while we were in the room with her (we still had to wear them elsewhere in the hospital).

Mom was awake. She was talking. She seemed "all there," more or less. She laughed. She mostly made sense. But she kept telling us that she was dying.

Rebecca and I, of course, assured her that she wasn't. That yes, Covid made you miserable, but that she was in good hands and would pull through.

For several days in a row, we repeated this scene.

Sometimes my brother was there. Sometimes Rebecca was with me. Sometimes I was there alone.

Mom went downhill fast. She mostly mumbled; maybe one in every ten sentences was intelligible.

After Mom had been in the hospital for a week, I received a phone call from one of her doctors. I can remember that we were on our way out the door – myself, my husband, and the younger kids, though I can't remember where we were going – and I stopped in the mudroom, gesturing for everyone else to go on out to the car while I took the call. I can remember the noise of the dryer running in the background as I sat on the back stairs and listened to the voice on the other end of the line.

Things were not going well. This was a shock to me, considering that everything I had heard up to that point was that Mom was sick but stable. This doctor was talking about more extreme measures, about ventilators and new medications and I can't even remember what else.

Her kidneys were shutting down. There was a medication they could give her to try to help, but they would have to give it to her via a tube down her throat. When they had spoken to her about it the day before, she had expressed that she did not want it. Now she had declined so much that they didn't feel they could discuss it with her again; she was not mentally able to make decisions for herself. Mom had listed me as her emergency contact and next-of-kin. The decisions fell to my brother and me.

They needed an answer. Then. Right away.

I was panicked, sitting alone next to the dryer, and I felt the sudden crushing weight of such a decision.

I asked them how long it would take for this last-ditch-effort medication to show results. They said they would know if it was working within forty-eight hours.

I told them to do it, but only for the forty-eight hours. If it wasn't helping, take the tube out.

Forty-eight hours did nothing for her.

The tube was removed. The bag attached to her catheter slowly filled with dark red fluid; I tried not to look at it, or think about it.

Mom's already frail frame wasted away further. Her hair, already thin from so many years of ill health, thinned even more, at an alarming rate. She stopped breathing on her own; the sound of the ventilator was a constant companion in those interminable hours I sat beside her.

After five days of unconsciousness, the doctors and nurses pulled my brother and I into the nearby conference room to discuss things.

She was not getting better. She was not likely to ever get better. Her body was shutting down, one organ at a time. They could do things to keep those organs functioning, but the chance of her body ever sustaining itself again was next to zero.

What did we want them to do?

I knew exactly what needed to be done. Mom and I had discussed it many times, sitting out there in the rocking chairs on my front porch.

She didn't want life-saving measures. She'd been miserable for the last decade, weak and tired and unhealthy. She had no desire to be kept here on earth longer than she had to be.

My brother and I asked the few questions we had. We discussed the decision together briefly; I told him what Mom had said to me, multiple times.

We told the doctors that we would cease all treatment. We did ask for a few days, so that everyone who wanted to come up and see Mom one last time would have the chance to do just that.

I let everyone know, via phone calls and social media, that we would be removing Mom from the ventilator that coming weekend. My brother and I made plans; we would split one full day with her ourselves. I had an afternoon and evening. He took the next morning. I came up early that afternoon, and that's when we opened things up for other people to visit. Uncles, aunts, cousins, and friends came by. My kids – the ones old enough to be allowed on the ward – came to say their goodbyes. There was a lot of standing around, talking in quiet tones, sharing memories. There was both laughter and tears.

During my hours alone with Mom, I brought up my laptop, set it up as close to her pillow as I could, and watched her favorite movie with her – *The Wizard of Oz* – holding her hand and gently touching her face, brushing her thin, tangled hair back. I sang along with Judy Garland about a land somewhere over the rainbow, and I cried as I said goodbye to my mother.

I have no idea if she could hear the sounds of that movie, or if she knew I was there at all. I like to think she could, and she did.

The time came. It was supposed to be just my brother and I there in the room with her, but my best friend had come up shortly before and asked if she could be allowed to stay as well, both as support for me and because Mom had been kind of a second mother to her. I asked my brother; he didn't mind.

We had asked beforehand what to expect. The doctors said it could take up to a day or two for her body to completely shut down; she'd be on medication the whole time that would assure she felt no pain. They said sometimes it could be a disturbing thing to watch when the actual moment came, that some patients would gasp and grimace and fight.

We were prepared – as much as we could be – for the worst.

What we got was something else entirely.

The room was startlingly quiet with the machines turned off. I sat on one side of the bed, holding Mom's hand, smoothing her hair back, and whispering to her that it was okay to let go. My best friend sat on the other side, one hand on Mom's arm. My brother stood and paced at the end of the bed.

It took fifteen minutes.

Fifteen quiet, calm, peaceful minutes in which her heart rate slowed little by little and her blood pressured dropped. Her breaths – shallow but easy – grew further and further apart.

And then everything simply stopped.

She was gone.

We sat with her for another hour until the men from the funeral home arrived, quiet and respectful.

I combed the tangles from her hair as best I could. I made calls to Mom's brother, one or two cousins. I let everyone else know on social media.

I hugged my brother and my best friend.

I went home.

We had Mom cremated; her memorial service was a month later, just a few days before the launch of my second book.

Looking back at that book now, it's strange to remember that at least half of it was written throughout 2022 while sitting in hospital rooms with my mom. I had so wanted it to be published while she was still around to see it. The book – *Tales My Grandmother Told Me* – was something of a family collection. I doubt I'll ever feel as personally connected to any other book I write as I do to that one.

But I digress.

Mom was gone.

And I began to do a lot of thinking.

Or rather, I began to let all the things I'd stopped myself from thinking for years finally have their time in the sun.

I was not happy with my own life. I hadn't been happy in a very long time.

Now, don't get me wrong. I wasn't miserable. I wasn't abused, or mistreated, or unloved. Life just… wasn't what I wanted. I had known that for a long time. And my mother's death made me really, truly face that fact for the first time.

You see, my mother *was* miserable. Not just physically; she had been unhappy with her own life for years before her cancer diagnosis and all the myriad problems that followed it.

There were a great number of reasons for this unhappiness. The greatest, looming over all the rest, was that she was still madly, desperately, unhealthily in love with my father, whom she had been divorced from for nearly twenty years. She had married a string of men – increasingly unattractive men, both physically and personality-wise – after my father. She was so desperate for connection, so needy, so completely unable to make decisions for herself, that she would latch on to the first man who showed her attention.

Until that man got fed up with her. Then she'd latch on to the next one.

She never loved any of them. She didn't want to love them. She wanted only safety, security – not in a financial way, but in a strange way where she felt like she wasn't a whole person without a partner.

I understand that part, I really do. I am also a person made for connection. It was the disconnect, the lack of love she felt for any of these men, the way she chose men who she *knew* she would never love – because if she didn't love them, they couldn't hurt her, that made the whole thing so unhealthy.

My mother also had the unfortunate habit of being *too* nice. She was nice to people she couldn't stand, just to avoid making waves or ever hurting people's feelings. One main example of this springs immediately to my mind.

We knew a woman who has spent her entire life *also* miserable – bitter, envious, and hateful. She is not an easy person to be around – never has been, but Mom could fake niceness with the best of them.

Mom wouldn't even call the woman by her name when she talked about her. She had a couple of things she called her, but I won't repeat them here. Mom would be mortified to have people know she talked that way. (I just got the best laugh, thinking of her reaction if anyone ever knew.) But she was always nice to her face. Always listened, always gave advice, always tried to help, while all the time secretly not being able to stand this woman.

The point being: Mom would be nice to people even when she couldn't stand them. Why? Because to not be nice might upset them, or might upset other people she *did* care about, who were close to the person. It was a strange sort of two-facedness, in which Mom could be a kind of martyr, bestowing gracious niceness on people to their faces yet despising them behind their backs, and still feel like she did it all for the sake of being *good*.

But relationships – romantic or otherwise – weren't the only thing that made her unhappy.

She'd spent her whole life doing nothing of note. I spoke about this in the eulogy I gave at her memorial service – I spun it in such a way that I could act like her lack of accomplishment was okay because her family loved her and she had done a lot of work in the church over the years, impacting lives in that way.

But inside… inside me something desperate and frantic was trying to speak up, to tell me something important.

I spent the next month thinking through all those things that I'd been pushing down inside me for so long. My own unhappiness. My mother's. The terrifying and disheartening idea that I might end up just like her, thirty or forty years down the road: a loveless, romanceless marriage; a life devoted to nothing but my children, with no real sense of myself beyond them; dying without having made any sort of mark on the world, no contribution worth remembering outside a small circle of family and friends.

I had been unhappy in my own marriage for many years. After a disastrous and traumatic relationship in my teens with the father of my first child, I had done exactly as my mother had: I had sought out a man who felt *safe*. Not safe in the way that I knew he would always protect me, physically and emotionally. No, safe in that I knew he was not the kind of man I would ever fall so desperately head-over-heels in love with that he would be able to break my heart.

I had lived in this way, in this relationship, for over two decades. Not miserable, but not truly happy. Comfortable, but not excited. Not waking up next to a man who made my heart flutter. Not in the throes of any kind of passionate lovemaking, not deep in intellectual, philosophical conversation.

I did it to myself, I'm well aware. I disciplined myself into the perfect, good, conservative Christian stay-at-home mom, housewife, homeschooler that best fit what made my husband happy.

And in the end, I hated myself for it.

I love my children immensely. I would kill for them, die for them, do anything in my power to show them love and help them on their way toward happiness. I felt for years that sacrificing my own desire for love and happiness was the best way to do that (there's that martyr syndrome rearing its ugly head again).

I had been nice to people that I couldn't stand. I had denied my own desires for the sake of making other people feel better. I had lived in a world which was someone else's fantasy. And the worst thing was that I had built that fantasy around myself, even though it wasn't my own. I had adopted a *well, it's not what I want, but it's what I've got, so I'll make the best of it* attitude.

I had buried myself in the grave of a life that I had dug myself.

I faced the horrible truth: I was fast on my way to becoming my mother. She was around my age when she started suffering horrible depression and anxiety, and started disassociating. She was my age when she finally, completely, gave up.

I didn't want to give up.

I wanted a life that made me happy.

And if I wanted to do that, I was going to have to be selfish for once.

Some major changes were going to happen.

It wasn't easy. None of it was. I'd spent half my life avoiding confrontation of any kind in order to keep a peace I didn't even want. Now I had to face up to things.

I had to ask my husband for a divorce.

The fact that it hit him like a bag of bricks dropping from the heavens is testament to how well I had faked it all over the years.

He wasn't a bad man. He had never mistreated me in any way. He just wasn't what I needed or wanted.

Telling our children was even harder. The older children either cried or took on looks of stoic disapproval. The younger ones had complete meltdowns.

We told various family members next. His family, mostly. They were supportive, truly, in a *you're both adults and your decisions are your own and we love you both whatever you do* kind of way.

I told my brother.

He was upset with me.

This would come to be a common theme. Even most of my own family would side with my soon-to-be ex-husband.

Well, the dissolution of our marriage was my fault. I asked for it. I knew I'd have to take that blame.

That didn't make it any easier.

We "separated," by which I mean that he moved into the bedroom across the hall. We thought this arrangement would be a good way to transition the kids from the world they had known to one in which their parents lived separate lives. Looking back now, I question whether that was the best way to do things. Hindsight is 20/20, right?

We began the paperwork for the divorce proceedings.

We both began to date.

I "dated" (online – long distance) a fellow writer for a few months. I traveled to his home, a few states away, and spent two weeks there with him. I thought it went well, but almost immediately afterward he started to pull away.

He was also a good guy, but he wasn't ready for a relationship. We spent the next couple of months in a sort of slow break-up, going more and more days without speaking, until finally the day came when he – and then I – admitted that we should stop trying.

I was strangely okay with this. I had seen it coming. I'd had time to prepare.

I felt stronger than I'd ever felt before. I had cried many times over those last couple of months, but I knew I could handle it. He didn't have enough power over me to destroy me.

And that's how I knew he wasn't the one.

He was a good steppingstone, though, a halfway point between what I'd had for twenty years and what I really, truly wanted.

That man would come along soon enough.

Joshua Daughrity. A blip on the screen of my life nearly a year prior, this man would turn out to be everything – every, comma, thing – I had ever wanted in a man.

Tall and handsome, with dark, silver-streaked hair and the most beautiful yet masculine hands I've ever seen. Ridiculously intelligent, and beyond that, truly wise. Ambitious and driven, yet humble and utterly kind.

Strong both physically, mentally, and emotionally. Creative and clever and funny. A writer with the ability to craft such huge, sweeping epic tales full of brilliance and love and heartbreak and courage and powerful storytelling that he blew me away immediately.

Completely masculine in all the good ways, which helped me come to terms with my own feminine energy. I *like* being a woman. I like feeling protected and provided for.

But I also like being respected for more than just – as my *new* husband says – blow jobs and baked goods.

What I needed was to be able to be a strong, intelligent, creative, successful woman while still feeling like my man was a leader who I could follow and who would keep me safe – in the good way. I had never had that before. My strength would have crushed my first husband, so I had always kept myself weak so as not to emasculate him.

But Josh – my strength will never be a problem to him. He is strong enough and secure enough in himself to not be threatened by anything I do.

Together, we are accomplishing amazing things.

But it hasn't been all sunshine and roses. I've done some things that pushed my older children away. They have not yet come to that point in life when they realize that their parents are people, too, people with hopes and dreams and fears and emotions all their own which have nothing to do with their children.

They have not yet reached the point where they can extend grace to their parents and understand that everyone, even Mom, is just trying their best to get through this life with the least misery possible.

I hope one day they'll come around.

I have lost friends.

My brother and sister-in-law have joined forces with Josh's ex-girlfriends to talk badly about us.

I find myself strangely unperturbed by this. My sister-in-law and I have had a rocky relationship since we were teenagers (picture me, for years, following in my mom's footsteps and being fake-nice for the sake of not rocking the boat – no more!), so I stopped caring about her opinion a very long time ago.

I had hoped for more from my brother, though. While I was not truly surprised by his choices, I was still disappointed.

But, through it all, I have *found* many things.

The true love of my life.

My place in the world as a writer, editor, and publisher.

The friends who were truly there for *me*, not some imagined version of me they had in their heads.

New friends. Funny, creative, smart, kind ones.

Most importantly: myself. That one is still a work in progress, and I think it may always be, because I think maybe it *should* be. Finding my own voice, allowing myself my own thoughts and opinions, breaking out of ridiculous assumptions and pressures put on me by both others and myself.

The first thing Josh taught me was to always be kind, but stop being so *nice*. Through his love and wisdom, along with a lot of self-reflection and dealing with cognitive dissonance, I am learning that it's okay to take up space in the world.

That it's okay to love those who deserve that love, to love myself, and most importantly, to not lose myself in the loving of others.

That's it's okay to expand my horizons, experience new things, and stop being so afraid all the time.

That it's okay to make mistakes and own them, to take chances because you never know what amazing things might come from them.

My mother died a year and a half ago.

I've made decisions and life changes since then that have had many people from my old existence questioning whether I've lost my mind completely.

And in a way, I can understand their concern. It seems like I've become an entirely different person.

But I haven't, not really. I've just finally let the real me come out and breathe.

And that's a decision that I'm okay with, no matter what anyone else thinks.

That's a decision that I think my mother and grandmother would have been quite proud of.

This work of fiction was formatted using 11-point Times New Roman font, the author's favorite, with 1.15 line spacing, on 55lb cream stock paper. The page size is 5.06" x 7.81." The custom margins are industry standard, 0.5" all around, and 0.00" inside, with no bleed, and 0.635" gutter, with mirrored margins.

Headers and footers are standard.

The cover is full color paperback in a matte finish.

The binding is 'perfect.'